What thou seest when thou dost wake,
  Do it for thy true-love take. . . .

—*WILLIAM SHAKESPEARE, A Midsummer Night's Dream*

Criss Cross

Criss Cross

by Lynne Rae Perkins

Greenwillow Books
An Imprint of HarperCollins *Publishers*

Criss Cross
Copyright © 2005 by Lynne Rae Perkins
All rights reserved. No part of this book may be used or reproduced in any manner whatsoever without written permission except in the case of brief quotations embodied in critical articles and reviews. Printed in the United States of America. For information address HarperCollins Children's Books, a division of HarperCollins Publishers, 1350 Avenue of the Americas, New York, NY 10019.
www.harperchildrens.com

The text of this book is set in Caslon 540.
Book design by Sylvie Le Floc'h

Library of Congress Cataloging-in-Publication Data
Perkins, Lynne Rae.
Criss Cross / by Lynne Rae Perkins.
    p.   cm.
"Greenwillow Books."
Summary: Teenagers in a small town experience new thoughts and feelings, question their identities, connect, and disconnect as they search for the meaning of life and love.
ISBN-10: 0-06-009272-6 (trade bdg.) ISBN-13: 978-0-06-009272-6 (trade bdg.)
ISBN-10: 0-06-009273-4 (lib. bdg.) ISBN-13: 978-0-06-009273-3 (lib. bdg.)
[1. Identity—Fiction.] I. Title.
PZ7.P4313Cr 2005 [Fic]—dc22 2004054023

First Edition 10 9 8 7 6 5

Greenwillow Books

For my loved ones

Special thanks to Bill, Frank and Lucy, my mom and Bob,
Tina and Pat at the Library, Mary at the Business Helper,
Anne the medical consultant, Michael J., who loaned me his guitar,
Pat I. the guitar consultant, Ben W. the chord player, Frank und
Soozie, Leigh and her friend Brian who knows about motorcycles.
And thanks to Virginia who knows about all kinds of things.

the spectrum of connectedness:

0%   100%

No one is
here—
no one.

No one
is
here—
no one.

people move back and forth in this
area like molecules in steam

Criss Cross

Contents

CHAPTER 1
The catch

She wished something would happen.

She wished it while she was looking at a magazine.

The magazine was her sister Chrisanne's; so was the bed she was sitting on and the sweater Debbie had decided to borrow after coming into Chrisanne's room to use her lip gloss. Chrisanne wasn't there. She had gone off somewhere.

Thinking she should be more specific in case her

wish came true, even though it wasn't an official wish, it was just a thought, Debbie thought, I wish something different would happen. Something good. To me.

As she thought it, she wound her finger in the necklace she was wearing, which was her own, then unwound it again. It was a short necklace, and she could only wrap her finger in it twice. At least while it was still around her neck.

The article she was looking at was about how the most important thing was to be yourself. Although the pictures that went with it recommended being someone else. Looking at them together made it seem like you could do both at the same time.

Debbie checked her wish for loopholes, because of all those stories about wishes that come true but cause disasters at the same time. Like King Midas turning his daughter and all of his food into gold. Even in her own life, Debbie remembered that once, when she was little, she had shouted that she wished everyone would just leave her alone. And then everyone did.

The trouble with being too careful about your wishes, though, was that you could end up with a wish so shapeless that it could come true and you wouldn't even know it, or it wouldn't matter.

She wrapped the necklace around her finger again, and this time it popped loose, flinging itself from her neck onto a bright, fuzzy photograph of a boy and a girl, laughing, having fun against a backdrop of sparkling water.

Debbie picked up her necklace and jiggled the catch.

stuck

It stuck sometimes in a partly open position, and the connecting loop could slip out.

Something like that, she thought, looking at the photo. Wondering if it would require being a different person.

In a way that doesn't hurt anyone or cause any natural disasters, she added, out of habit.

Fastening the chain back around her neck, trying to tell by feel whether the catch had closed, she thought of another loophole. Hoping it wasn't too late to tack on one more condition, she thought the word *soon*.

The wish floated off, and she turned the page.

CHAPTER 2

Hector Goes into a Sponge State and Has a Satori

Meanwhile, in another part of town, Hector's sister, Rowanne, was upstairs in her bedroom, changing her clothes or something. Hector could hear her humming, and the sound of drawers opening and closing.

He was crossing the front hall on his way to the kitchen and, as he passed the mirror, he glanced in and gave himself a little smile. It was something he always did; he didn't know why. For encouragement, maybe.

This time he smiled hello at himself just as a

slanted ray of sun shot through one of the diamond-shaped windows in the front door at the side of his face, producing a sort of side-lit, golden, disembodied-head effect in the mirror. It struck him as an improvement on the usual averageness of his face; it added some drama. Some intrigue. An aura of interestingness his sister's face had all the time, but his did not, which mystified him because when he compared their features one at a time, a lot of them seemed identical. Or almost identical. There were some small differences. Like their hair. Their hair was different.

They both had auburn hair, but while Rowanne's auburn hair plummeted in a serene, graceful waterfall to her waist, Hector's shot out from his head in wiry, dissenting clumps.

And while both of their faces were slim, freckled ovals with a hint of roundness, Hector's was rounder. Rowanne had slipped away from her roly-poly childhood like a sylph from a cocoon, but Hector's was still wrapped around him in a soft, wooly layer.

Their eyes were blue-gray, behind almost identical

wire-rimmed glasses resting on very similar slender noses. But Rowanne's eyes-glasses-nose constellation somehow conveyed intelligence and warmth. Hector's conveyed friendly and goofy. Why? What was the difference? Maybe it was his eyes, he was thinking. Maybe they were too close together. Maybe they would move farther apart as he matured, like a flounder's. Although when he thought about it, he seemed to remember that both the flounder's eyes ended up on the same side of its face. He tried to remember what made that happen, if it was something the flounder did, and if maybe he could do the opposite. Perhaps it would help that he wasn't lying on the bottom of the ocean watching for food to float by.

He definitely felt unfinished, still in process. He felt that there was still time, that by the time three years had passed and he was seventeen, as Rowanne was now, he, too, might coalesce into something. Maybe not something as remarkable as Rowanne, but something. It was possible, he felt.

Hector took off his glasses to see if his eyes

looked better without them. He looked blurrier, which seemed to heighten the cinematic, enigmatic quality lent by the falling sun's sideways glance. His clumpy hair dissolved softly into the shadows, and the effort he had to make to see gave an intense, piercing quality to his gaze. Maybe corrected vision wasn't all it was cracked up to be. Maybe in ancient times, when distinct edges were unknown to many people, he would have been considered handsome. Though he might have had a lot of headaches.

The sun dropped a degree and the golden disembodied moment passed. Hector put his glasses back on and was about to turn away when a sharp jab of weight on his shoulder made him jump. It was Rowanne's chin. She had sneaked up behind him, and her face appeared next to his in the mirror. So much like his, but more. There was just no explaining it.

Rowanne smiled, and they both turned and headed for the kitchen. Rowanne was ahead of him, and Hector noticed she had a piece of the newspaper in her hand.

"Do you want to go somewhere with me?" she asked.

"Where?" asked Hector. Their parents had already gone out for the evening. He didn't know what Rowanne's plans were, but his were to call out for pizza and watch movies on TV.

"A coffeehouse thing," she said. "It's at Arland Community College. In Arland."

She unfolded the newspaper on the kitchen table and pointed to a small advertisement.

"See?" she said. "Do you want to go?"

Hector looked at the ad. A couple of questions came to mind. The main one was, why was she asking him to go along, why didn't she just call one of her bezillion friends? But he didn't bring it up because she didn't often invite him along and he didn't want her to change her mind. He thought he might like to go. He had never been to a coffeehouse thing or, for that matter, a college. It sounded kind of interesting.

"I really, really think we should go," said Rowanne. As if it had just occurred to her.

"Okay," he said. "Sure. Why not?"

The parking lot they pulled into at dusk was half empty. Or half full, Hector was thinking. As if to welcome them, a half-dozen lights on tall poles flickered to life. In the thirty minutes it had taken them to drive there, the air had slipped from almost-spring back to still-winter. Stepping out of the overheated car, Hector found himself shivering. He zipped up his flimsy nylon windbreaker and pulled the drawstring of the small hood snugly around his face, although he knew this made him look like a turtle without its shell. He alternated between warming his hands in his armpits and forcing them down into the pockets of his jeans.

A few more cars pulled in and released noisy gusts of people into the chilly air. Car doors slammed. Hector noticed that the newcomers were braving the cold without headgear, and he pulled the skimpy hood back off. It was colder this way, but he felt it made him look older. Colder but older. Older but colder. Colder and colder, older and older.

The edge of night moved visibly across the sky.

The other people swarmed from the parking lot up onto a sidewalk and down a trail of evenly spaced pools of light. Minutes passed. Hector bounced up and down on his heels to keep warm. Finally Rowanne got out of the car (what was she doing in there, anyway?) and they, too, headed down the trail of bright, softly buzzing circles.

The sidewalk led to a courtyard set between several buildings, the chief distinguishing feature of which was that you couldn't tell them apart. They were concrete and modern, but followed the medieval practice of having small, recessed slits of windows that arrows could be shot out of but which would be difficult to shoot arrows into. They seemed to have been designed for easy cleaning with a hose and a giant squeegee, like the concrete stalls at the Humane Society.

It didn't fit Hector's idea of what a college should be like. He realized that his ideas about colleges came mostly from movies. He knew the difference between movies and real life, but he thought that at least some of the movies must have been filmed on location, or be based on real places. The movie colleges tended to have ivy-covered brick walls and massive old oaks. They had big grassy lawns, and they seemed like places where a human might like to spend some time. He looked at the concrete planters that held only dirt and stray wads of paper, bordered by concrete benches and installed at equal intervals across the concrete plaza. Maybe it looked better in the daytime, in sunlight. Or blanketed by snow. Or in total darkness. The only humanizing influence was the humans, crisscrossing the court in chattering bunches. They seemed to be in pretty high spirits, though. Controlled substances, he was guessing.

He heard Rowanne calling his name and realized that he had stopped walking. She hurried back and led him by his elbow to a glass door.

"How do you know where you're going?" he asked. "Have you been here before?"

"Maybe once or twice," said Rowanne.

The room they entered was dimly lit and crowded. Candles in red glass globes lit circles of faces at each table. Voices bounced around the painted concrete block walls before being sucked into the acoustical ceiling tile. Dark brown beams and worn orange carpeting had been glued on here and there to suggest warmth and atmosphere.

Hector and Rowanne paused. A flurry of waving hands and a couple of shouts drew them toward a table on the far side of the room. They waded through hip-high thickets of occupied plastic chairs, some of which inched apart to make a passageway while others remained unmoved, leaving narrow canyons only a wasp could thread. Hector tried to psychically compress his girth since, compared to a wasp, he was more like a camel.

The table, when they got there, was filled with

Rowanne's friends. A single empty chair waited for Rowanne, and a thought whispered from the back of Hector's mind, but it was drowned out by the sounds of scraping, shifting chairs.

There wasn't quite enough room for Hector's chair. His chair was a peninsula, jutting out into the nonexistent space between tables, in the position where a dog might sit to wait patiently for scraps. At least he had a chair, though. Unlike the dog.

His right knee touched the southwest corner of Rowanne's chair, and his left knee touched the southeast edge of the chair of Rowanne's best friend, Liz. A dark, trapezoidal chasm yawned between his knees and the table where, next to the red candle, there was a plastic basket filled with peanuts. Hector had to stand up and lean over to grab some. He grabbed with both hands to cut down on how often he would have to do it. He had a feeling this might be his main entertainment for the evening. He emptied the peanuts into his lap and cracked one open, then wondered what he should do with the shells. He looked around to see what other people were doing with theirs, and settled on piling them neatly on the edge of the table.

Eating the peanuts made him thirsty.

Someone carrying two cups of hot coffee squeezed behind Hector's chair in a series of forceful sideways thrusts. The hot coffee tended, because of the principle of inertia, to remain where it was even when the cups moved on, so that with each thrust, splats of hot, homeless coffee fell (gravity) onto Hector's shoulder, his head, his other shoulder.

His good humor began to waver a little. He found himself thinking fondly of home: the couch. The television. The front door that you opened to receive the fragrant pizza.

But then a friend of Rowanne's named Chip or Skip (or was it Flip?) set a paper cup of brown pop down in front of Hector. Rowanne's friend Liz scooted her chair back so that Hector could pull forward and sit almost next to her. A guy with a guitar climbed onto the stage and started plunking out chords that dropped softly into the noise of the room, making pockets of quiet wherever they fell. Hector was drawn gently back into the evening.

"So," he said to Liz, relaxing slightly in his chair, "do you come here often?"

He was just asking for information, but she laughed and Hector realized it sounded like something different, like something a man would say to a woman in a movie. A pickup line. He flushed a little, but it was okay. It was dark, and it was just Liz.

The guitarist on the stage, tuning his guitar, let pure drops of sound fall into the noisy room, making the pockets of quiet. The drops fell into the middle of conversations and hushed them. The drops of sound fell on an unmoistened sponge that was waiting somewhere inside Hector. In his heart or his mind or his soul. He didn't realize that he was in a sponge state but, having been separated from his moorings— couch, TV, pizza—and led into unfamiliar territory, there was a spongy piece of him left open and receptive to the universe in whatever form it might take, and the form it took was a guitar.

Hector's first thought about the guitar was how good it sounded. It sounded great. There was something different about it than a radio or a record. There was more darkness and more brightness to it. And the guy who was playing it was amazing. He had finished tuning by now and was picking out a jumpy, catchy little tune.

He didn't look like a person who would be an amazing guitar player. Or an amazing anything. Not at first. His apparent ordinariness helped a second thought to sprout on Hector's moistened sponge, which was that it didn't look that hard. Or maybe it was hard, but it looked like fun. It looked like the guy was having a blast.

The guitarist started to sing. The song was about his little chicken, whose name is Marie and who don't like no one but him—"me" in the song, so it could rhyme with "Marie." It was a different kind of music than Hector ever listened to. Sort of hillbilly, he thought, but sort of something else, too. He liked it. There was something about it that he really liked.

He glanced over to see if Rowanne was paying attention. She was. She was paying so much attention you could cut it with a knife. She was rapt. He looked at Liz. She was rapt, too. He looked at the musician again, who didn't look so ordinary anymore. His music had transformed him, or revealed a part of him that was plugged into the cosmic life force. A life force that seeped in, through, and under the music, like God in the Communion wafer. An everyday kind of life force, though, that could do this in a song about a chicken. More about earth than heaven. Also, girls really liked it.

These aren't words that Hector thought. He wasn't even thinking in words. He was having a satori, a mystical, wordless moment of under-standing about Music and Life, including the subcategory of the look on Rowanne's and Liz's faces, that passed through him and altered the shape of his thoughts like water through a sandstone cavern. Like water on a dry sponge.

It's hard to say how long the moment lasted, but when it was gone, Hector knew that he wanted to learn to play the guitar.

He said so to Liz, during a pause between songs. She smiled and said, "That's a great idea. You should do it."

Liz was a nice person who said nice things. She had a way of making them sound true.

With each performer who followed, even the ones Hector didn't think were that good, the idea grew stronger in his mind. By the time the fluorescent lights flickered on overhead, it was a fact to him. A fact that made the world more alive and more interesting. More promising.

People were standing up and putting coats on, there was a lot of chatter, and with all the dragging and colliding of chairs it was hardly even noticeable when Hector stood up and his lapful of forgotten peanuts cascaded to the floor. He had to walk on them to get around to the back of his chair. As he made his treacherous way over the rolling, crunching shells, he heard Chip/Skip/Flip say that everyone was going (somewhere, Hector didn't catch that part), and was Rowanne coming? And he heard Rowanne say, "I can't, I promised my parents I'd bring Hector home right afterward." Inwardly, Hector snorted. Outwardly, he tried to look like someone who needed to be taken home.

In the car on the way home, Hector and Rowanne were quiet for a while, waiting for the heater to kick in. Hector positioned his feet over the two holes in the floor, to keep the heat from whooshing directly from the vent to the outside. It was a dark night, and Rowanne was a tentative driver. Being in a car with her as she felt her way over the winding back roads was like being inside a flashlight held by someone searching for a contact lens.

"So," she said, after a while, "did you like it?"

"Yeah," said Hector. "I did. I liked it a lot. I think I liked the first guy the best."

"Yeah," said Rowanne. "He's really good."

"How long do you think it takes to learn to play like that?" asked Hector.

Rowanne allowed her eyes to leave the road for a microsecond to glance at him.

"I don't know," she said. "Years, probably. You better get started right away."

She relaxed as they moved into the streetlight-lit streets of Birdvale, then under the railway trestle into Seldem.

Hector said, "So, I'm not mad or anything, I'm glad I went, but why didn't you just tell me you needed me for an excuse not to go out with Chip-Dip?"

"Skip," said Rowanne. "I'm sorry. That was stupid. But would you have come?"

"I don't know," said Hector. "Maybe. I would go now, though. Now that I know what it's like."

When they reached their driveway, it was empty. So was the house. Their parents were still off somewhere. The lamps they had left on had lit up quiet, empty rooms all evening.

There was some leftover ham in the fridge. They started cutting it into chunks and dipping it into a custard cup full of French dressing. The Swiss cheese dipped in mustard was also very good.

"How come you don't like Skip?" asked Hector. "He seems all right." He went to a cupboard and found an open can of mixed nuts. Rowanne went to the fridge again and searched the shelves inside the door. She selected a tall, skinny jar of olives and the mayonnaise.

"He's all right," she said. "He's just not—"

She paused to think. Hector stopped chewing. If Rowanne said something important, something he needed to know, he didn't want to miss it.

"He's just not my type," she said.

"Oh," said Hector. He had been looking for something more specific. For insight into the female mind. He was a little disappointed. But Rowanne wasn't finished.

"He looks at me with cow eyes," she said. "I sort of liked it at first. But now it makes me want to slap him upside the head."

"Wow," said Hector. "That seems harsh."

"It's just an expression," said Rowanne. "I wouldn't really slap him. I don't think."

"What kind of eyes should he look at you with?" asked Hector.

"I think just human eyes would be all right," said Rowanne.

The next day was a Saturday. The air was soft and sun warmed and called out for some reckless act of liberation. Hector hacked the legs off a pair of jeans and put them on.

He had to help his dad take down the storm windows and put up the screens. All the while Hector was thinking about the guitar idea. He wasn't thinking about the practical part, of how he could actually do it. He was just thinking of how it had made him feel.

After dinner he headed out to walk to his friend Phil's house. He saw tiny pink buds and blossoms erupting from sodden black limbs. A winter's worth of trash unfolding from shrunken icy lumps of charcoal-colored snow. Voices floated toward the sidewalk from the open windows of houses and from the windows of cars rolling by on the gritty street, real voices and radio voices, from windows that only yesterday had been shut tight. The balmy, sunny day had coaxed them open.

The warmth was slipping into coolness as Hector stepped off the curb to cross Pittsfield Street, and as he headed up Prospect Hill Road he heard a few windows thud shut. But he still felt as if the world was opening, like the roof of the Civic Arena when the sky was clear.

Life was rearranging itself; bulging in places, fraying in spots. Sometimes leaving holes big enough to see through, or even step through, to somewhere else.

He waved to a couple of girls he knew, across the street. Their lips were shiny, their arms were folded in front of them, sheets of hair swayed gently behind like a hypnotist's pocket watch, in a way that was related to how they moved as they walked. They were changing from caterpillars into butterflies. Hector felt himself changing, too, but into what? Not a butterfly.

All he could think of was a dog. Friendly, loyal, with shiny eyes. They're changing into butterflies, he thought, and I'm changing from a puppy into a young dog. Could that go anywhere?

Two more butterflies materialized on the sidewalk a few houses ahead. Hector trailed behind them for a while at a respectful distance, lost in his thoughts. Until he realized that he had missed his turnoff and was going the wrong way.

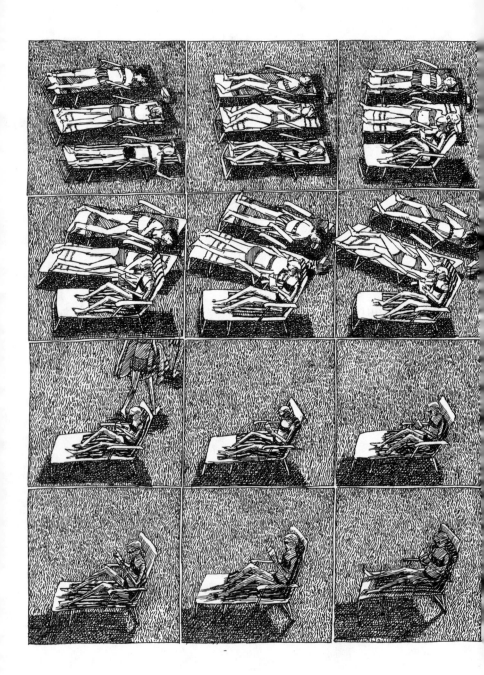

CHAPTER 3

Boys, Dogs, Science Fiction

Debbie and Chrisanne and their neighbor Tesey lay prostrate on their chaise lounges. It was the first really good laying-out day of the season. They had a radio and wet glasses with drinks full of melting ice. Every half hour or so they turned ninety degrees, like chickens roasting on invisible rotisseries. They also adjusted their orientation to the sun as it moved across the sky to allow its ultraviolet rays to be inflicted most directly and effectively.

After the third turn Debbie raised the back of her lounge chair so she could sit up, and opened a book she had brought out with her. She was immediately absorbed in reading, and sat motionless while Tesey and Chrisanne continued their quarter-turn rotations for a few more spins, then folded up their chairs to go inside.

One of them must have said something to her. The remnant of a question hung in the air, and she noticed they had paused, as if waiting.

"I'll be in in a minute," she said. But then she forgot about going in. She forgot about the sun and how it was scorching the front of her winter-pale thighs and shins, the tops of her shoulders and her nose and the skin where her hair was parted.

She stayed there all afternoon and came out again after dinner, this time in shorts and a sweatshirt, to finish the book. The backyard was now in the long evening shadow of the house. As the air cooled, she drew her legs up inside the sweatshirt. After she read the last page, she looked at the picture on the cover again, then tossed the book down onto the grass. Her arms withdrew from her sleeves and joined her legs inside the warm cavern of her sweatshirt.

It was a science fiction novel, about a planet in another solar system where all of the Beings have lived calmly and harmoniously for thousands of their years until some people from earth come along and screw it all up in about ten minutes by offering them an apple, which none of them had ever seen. The Beings had been gentle and peaceful. They had lived simply, but were very advanced. For example, they used mental telepathy. Their tunics, constructed somehow without any seams or fasteners, were made of a miracle fabric that kept them comfortable in any weather. The fabric was iridescent or gray, depending on whether or not you felt like telepathing. Everyone's tunic was equal but unique; you got one at birth and it grew right along with you. It had strands from your own DNA equivalent woven into it.

The whole planet was nutritionally complete; you could just grab a piece of anything and eat it. The bitten thing would then regenerate. (But they didn't have apples.)

What was it about the peaceful planet, Debbie wondered, that while it sounded beautiful and idyllic, also made her feel ornery and restless, made her want to turn up the music, eat burgers, and squirrel away mountains of material possessions while she still could? Maybe that's why the Beings rode their version of pogo sticks everywhere: to bounce out the rebellious urges.

She did think, though, that she would almost welcome the part about how the unseen, disembodied governing Wisdom assigned everyone a mate. It happened telepathically. You just knew.

Telepathy wasn't working for Debbie so far. She had felt the sudden just knowing, and had tried to casually but silently project her whole inner self or something, but the other parties, the objects of her sudden knowledge, had remained oblivious.

She knew that she would have to talk. She should have been able to do it. But she had developed a black hole in her brain. She could be in the middle of a normal conversation with a boy and the instant she thought of him that way—as a boy—the black hole sucked all her words away. Except for a few stupid ones. The stupid ones stayed in there.

She called to her dog, Cupcake, who was sitting in the grass a few feet away. He trotted over, and Debbie scratched him behind the ears and talked to him. It was easy. Cupcake found everything she had to say interesting and important. He wanted to hear more. Her neck-scratching transported him to a state of bliss; he offered her his throat for scratching, then his belly. If boys could be more like dogs, she thought. Or Beings.

CHAPTER 4
Radio Show

Hector was late, so Phil walked across the street to see what Lenny was doing with his dad's pickup truck in the driveway. It was moving forward and back, forward and back over the gravel. When Lenny saw Phil, he stopped and turned off the engine, but he left the radio on and fiddled with the dial.

"Whatcha doing?" asked Phil.

"There's this weird radio show I heard last

week," said Lenny. "I think it's the right time for it to come on. Go around and get in."

As Phil came around the front of the pickup, he saw Debbie sitting in her backyard, and waved. She was scrunched up in a lawn chair, almost completely inside of her sweatshirt. The sleeves hung empty, and all that emerged from the lumpy gray cocoon was her head on top and her pointy sneakers from the bottom.

One of the sleeves came to life, and a hand popped out briefly and waved back.

Seeing Phil wave, Lenny said, "Is Debbie still over there? Tell her to come listen, too." Then he opened his door, hoisted up to a standing position, and told her himself, hollering over the roof of the truck.

Debbie slid to the middle of the long, benchy seat. Lenny sat behind the wheel, Phil leaned against the passenger side door with his elbow hanging out of the window. It was one of the more comfy places the three of them had sat since their mothers first propped them up in neighboring corners of the sandbox, watching them from lawn chairs to make sure they didn't tip over. More often they sat on concrete stoops or on the curb. On bike seats or in the grass. Sometimes kitchen chairs, but more often outside. They looked for one another when nothing else was happening, the way you pick up a magazine or look in the cupboard for a snack. Not exactly by accident and not exactly on purpose. You could go out into the world and do new things and meet new people, and then you could come home and just sit on the stoop with someone you had never not known, and watch lightning bugs blink on and off.

Debbie slid down on the worn vinyl until her elbows rested on the seat cushion and put her feet up on the cracked, dusty dashboard, forming her body into the shape of the Big Dipper. It was a relief to shift her thoughts away from boys and what happened when she tried to talk to one of them.

"So, what's this show?" she asked Lenny.

"Just listen," he said. "You'll like it."

The show was called "Criss Cross." It started off with a lot of songs that could be considered sick but could also be considered funny: "Poisoning Pigeons in the Park," "Don't Eat the Yellow Snow," and "Dead Skunk in the Middle of the Road." Some were more on the sick side, some were more on the funny side, and some were just off the wall. It was the kind of radio show you would like if you liked *Mad Magazine*. Which they all did, or had, a few years ago. There were comedy parts, too.

Hector appeared at Phil's window midway through the show and listened with them, leaning on the door. The show ended with a string of "What do you get when you cross a (something) with a (something else)?" jokes. Then there was what must have been a clip from an old movie, a male voice saying "Crisscross," followed by what sounded like a train wreck. That was it. A commercial came on, and Lenny flipped off the radio.

Debbie's feet were still propped up on the dashboard and, in their fronts-only sunburned state, her bare legs reminded Hector of a freshly opened, unscooped box of Neapolitan ice cream, minus the chocolate stripe.

"Nice tan," he observed.

Then he said, "What do you get when you cross a butterfly with a dog?"

"We give up," said Phil. "What?"

"I don't know," said Hector. "Probably nothing."

CHAPTER 5

Leg Buds

Hanging out in the truck listening to the radio show got to be a regular thing. It wasn't an official plan, but almost every Saturday night through the spring, and then the summer, they all showed up and sat there in the parked truck in Lenny's driveway, with the radio on.

Only three of them could actually sit inside the truck. The other two had to listen through the open windows, leaning against the doors. The fifth person was Debbie's friend Patty, who came the second week, and whenever she could after that. The first time she and Debbie walked over from Debbie's backyard, Hector and Phil were already sitting inside with Lenny, but immediately they slid out and offered up their seats.

This seemed unusual to Debbie. Then she realized that they were being chivalrous. Like gentlemen. Like men. A new part of them was emerging before her eyes, like leg buds bumping out on tadpoles.

Midway through the show, Debbie tested her theory by offering to trade places with Hector, who was leaning on the outside of the door beside her.

"No, no," he said. "That's okay. I'm fine. I like standing up. Leaning against a truck. For an hour."

A few minutes later he shifted his weight and said, "It's fun."

"What is?" asked Debbie.

"Standing up. Leaning against a truck," he said. "For an hour.

"I don't want to be selfish, though," he said after a pause. "If you wanted to have some fun, too, we could trade places for a while."

Debbie looked at him. He was smiling a winsome smile. A hopeful smile.

"Okay," she said, pulling on the handle, opening the door.

She smiled, too, as she swung her legs out and hopped down off the seat. Hector helped pull the door open and, as he stepped around it, Debbie landed with force on top of him, or at least on one of his feet, which was painful. There was a full frontal collision with vertical slippage as in the shifting of tectonic plates, and together they stepped one way, then the other, then back again, trying unsuccessfully to go around each other.

Finally, using a move he had learned from his mother, Hector put his right hand on the small of Debbie's back, took her right hand with his left, and spun her around and away, ballroom dancing style. In his mother's lessons his dancing partner had been

Rowanne, and he had gazed into his sister's chin. Now his gaze met Debbie's eyes. Inadvertently, but all the same. His mother had said this would happen.

Debbie's eyes looked surprised. Then they looked away. When they looked back, they had normalized. Normal eyes-ed. With the curtains drawn, at least partway.

"Sorry," she said. "About stepping on your foot. Is it okay?"

"It's okay," said Hector. "I kind of liked it."

He said it as a joke, but it wasn't entirely untrue.

Then he remembered that he was supposed to be getting in the truck.

So he did.

CHAPTER 6

In the Rhododendrons

Debbie and Patty stood inside a thriving mountain of rhododendrons, flowering with primeval abandon against a withered, sagging garage that was slowly subdividing into raw materials, basic elements and individual atoms on the edge of an oily, pothole-dotted forgotten cinder alley. The alley ran between the backsides of tall, uneven hedges that concealed parallel rows of backyards.

Across the alley from the rhododendrons, the

hedge was high enough that only the top bar of the swingset inside was visible. Between the rhododendrons and the old garage, a sort of room had formed, an arched, private space among the branches, tall enough to stand up in. Even when it was raining, as it was now, it stayed fairly dry there.

It was the perfect place to change your clothes on the way to school. You could drape the clothes you were taking off over the branches while you got the other ones on. Debbie stepped out of a pair of turquoise, white, and orange plaid double-knit bell-bottoms. Patty unbuttoned a flowered blouse and tossed it onto a branch that already sported a brown jumper. The air was warm. They stood on top of their shoes in their underwear, the rain softly piffing on the leaves all around. Two Eves in the Garden of Eden.

"If you think about it," Patty said, "it shouldn't even matter what we wear. People will like us for who we are."

Debbie knew this. She even believed it was true. But she also believed that certain articles of clothing could transmit almost impenetrable counter signals. Like camouflage.

"How will they know who I am if I'm wearing these?" she asked.

Patty laughed.

"They're all right," she said. "Sort of. They're better than a jumper."

"I think they're equal to a jumper," said Debbie. "Or less than. Jumpers can be okay."

The reason they were changing their clothes in a rhododendron bush was cultural evolution. Both of them had mothers who were stranded in the backwaters of a bygone era, and who were unable to grasp many current trends and ideas. You could argue and argue, but they weren't going to get it. At some point you just had to go change your clothes in a bush.

First, though, you had to acquire the clothes you wanted to change into, which were slightly faded bell-bottomed jeans that almost touched the ground, or did touch it, even dragging a little bit. And if you weren't yet financially independent, or had spent all your money on movies and pizza, you had to get your mother to buy them for you.

That could be hard.

It wasn't hard for Debbie to get her mother to go shopping. But Helen Pelbry was opposed to spending money on something that was going to drag on the ground and get ruined. She could not hear the siren call of the dragging jeans.

Debbie heard it. She believed that it was the only way to wear pants that made any sense. That wearing the dragging jeans did not actually guarantee that good things would happen to you, but not wearing them could almost guarantee that the good things wouldn't.

She felt sure that when she found the perfect pair, her mother would recognize their perfection and relent. But they weren't finding the perfect pair. They had been searching for hours, in every store in the airy, light-filled Merionville Mall. The fountains burbled, and sunlight poured in through the skylights, encouraging the tropical trees and flowers, but Debbie and her mother had become acutely focused on the two inches of the earth's atmosphere just above the carpet of the dressing room floor.

Though the jeans were wrong in other ways, too. It was almost dreamlike, how many ways they could be wrong in, ways that a person would not have imagined. They had wandered into quicksand, into a shopping swamp. A fog of fatigue and unreality crept up on Debbie. She could tell that her mother was getting exasperated, too. They stood close to each other in a tiny dressing room with the maximum number of items hanging from a hook on the wall. Debbie was wearing a unique pair of turquoise, white, and orange plaid bell-bottoms that hovered three inches from the floor. Her mother had found them.

"What's wrong with these?" she asked Debbie. Her voice was careful. Her face was composed, with a trace of hopefulness. Her purse dangled from the crook of her crisscrossed arms.

Debbie considered. She tried to be objective.

The plaid was all right, maybe, kind of, but the pants were so short, and they had a peculiar, zingy bell curve that would always be there because they were made of some miracle fiber that "remembered" its shape, washing after washing. It was amazing how wrong they were, but they did have a weird perfection, as objects. Not objects you would wear. Just objects you would look at. Like a vase. That was it, that was the shape. The shape of an upside-down, plaid vase. Or two of them, her feet blooming out on long stems.

Maybe her resolve was broken by some mild tranquilizing vapor seeping out of the ventilation vent along with the air-freshening perfume. Maybe there were subliminal messages in the upbeat, impersonal music softly emanating around the flimsy partitions. Maybe she just wanted her mother to be happy, and for them to be having a nice time together, the way they always had. Maybe it finally seemed stupid to care so much.

Debbie heard herself saying, "These are good. I really like these."

In the instant she said it, she almost believed it. She wanted it to be true. If she could have spent her whole life in the tiny private dressing room, she might have worn those pants a lot.

She said the same thing about the next pair she tried on, a pair of jeans with a machine-embroidered image, at the bottom of one leg, of a bunny nibbling on a bunch of carrots. In this case she had an ulterior motive. They were, by sheer accident or luck, the right length.

"I can hem them," she said, wondering why she hadn't thought of it before. She was fibbing, but it was a noble fib, because she was really saying, "I love you. I want us to be having fun." She was also saying, "If you really love me, you won't make me hem them."

But her mother only heard the words she said aloud. Her face relaxed. She looked pleased and relieved.

"You're sure?" she asked.

"They're great," said Debbie. "I like them a lot."

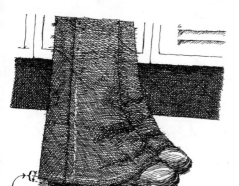

margin
of error:
about ¼"
either way

regular

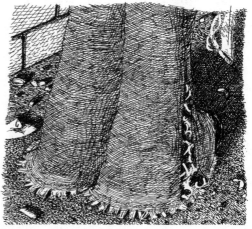

advanced

← words
spoken
while
in trance

← dressing room
miasma

other

In the hollow of the rhododendrons, Debbie and Patty used the seam rippers they had smuggled out of their mothers' sewing boxes. Debbie was carefully removing the bunny and the carrots, dropping bits of white and orange thread on the dirt. Patty was taking out the large hems she had sewed in her jeans the night before, like Penelope unraveling her weaving in the Odyssey, only backward and for different reasons.

"Maybe I can iron them out in the home ec room," she said. "So they hang down better."

"And then maybe you can smoosh them up so they're not all crispy," said Debbie.

"I don't care so much if they're crispy," said Patty. "Just so they're long enough."

While they were working, a pair of playful chipmunks chased each other through the branches, and a few fat robins, seeking refuge from the rain, now more a downpour than a drizzle, chirped. It felt very Arcadian, as if a shepherd might appear with a harp and some grapes.

What appeared instead was a car blasting down the alleyway, throwing up wild sprays of puddle water as it clunked in and out of potholes. The two girls froze, only their eyes moving, and remained hidden. In the noise and commotion, neither one noticed that behind them a startled chipmunk had jumped from a narrow limb to the ground. A slender gold chain was momentarily tangled around his front paws. He dragged it for a short distance before he got free of it and scampered away. It settled down into the neatly mowed grass of someone's backyard, in the rain, getting wet.

CHAPTER 7
The Fable of Lenny

At least the windows were open. Even so, the odor was thick and pungent. Debbie experimented with different methods of breathing. Nose only. Mouth only. Hand casually over nose. Nose casually over right shoulder, hunk of hair used casually as an air filter. She was looking for ways to inhale that would not make her want to gag. She tried pulling her T-shirt up over her nose. Probably the smell was something you could get used to. She was used to her dad's cigarettes, but Lenny's chewing tobacco had a sour, heavy mintiness suggestive of putting your nose in the armpit of someone who had applied scented deodorant after already having sweated.

Every now and then he leaned out of the window and spit.

"That stuff stinks," said Phil. "How can you stand having it in your mouth?"

"I like it," said Lenny.

He did like it, sort of. He was going to like it, once he got used to it. It had startled him, at first, to have the flavor inside his own mouth, but it was the taste of the smell of his father, and his father's friends. It was strange to him, but it was also friendly.

Debbie, between Lenny and Phil, breathed shallowly the aromas of laundered cotton and her own skin and scrutinized her bare feet, up on the dashboard. She had put decals on her toenails that afternoon, but she thought she might take them off later. They were the last set left in the package, and they weren't very good. All the good ones were used up. From any farther than six inches, these were just irregular black squiggles with some blurry blobs of purple and blue. It looked like she had banged her toes one at a time with a hammer. Lenny looked at them, too. He couldn't make out what they were. Dragonflies? Skull and crossbones?

"What are those on your toes?" he asked. "Are they supposed to be grapes?"

The lump in his cheek caused him to speak a little less clearly, as if he had a lump of something wedged between his gum and his cheek. Which he did.

"Fish," Debbie said to the inside of her T-shirt. "Tropical fish."

"Maybe you should just chew gum," suggested Phil. "Since when do you dip snuff, anyway?"

"The guy I work for over at the garage asked me if I wanted a pinch," said Lenny. "So I decided to try it.

"I like it," he said again. He was sticking to his story.

The garage where Lenny swept up a few hours a week, emptied trash, helped out, was run by a friend of his dad's. Sometimes Jerry let him do easy jobs, like changing oil and spark plugs. He could have done quite a bit more; he knew how. It seemed to Lenny as if he had always known how. Or could figure it out, if he didn't.

That's how he saw himself. Debbie and Phil saw him that way, too. They also saw another Lenny, though, inseparable from the current Lenny, the mechanical whiz dirt-bike Lenny. They saw the Lenny of their childhood. The bookworm Lenny.

The fable of Lenny was that when he was younger, he read encyclopedias for fun. . . .

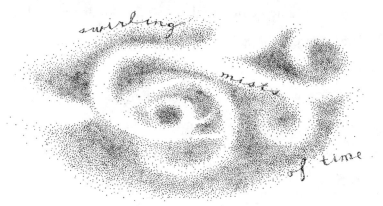

His mother, Edie, brought them home one at a time from the A&P. They were a promotional item, a new volume each week for $1.49 with a $20.00 purchase. She had already brought home a complete set of china this way, as well as stainless-steel flatware and Pyrex baking dishes.

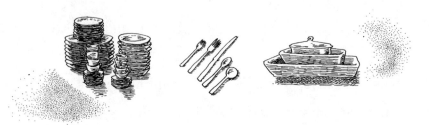

The encyclopedias were handsomely bound in brown leatherette and embossed with black and gold lettering. They came with a wooden shelf that held the entire set. Edie put them back on Lenny's dresser to get them out of her way.

Lenny watched as the shelf filled up with the elegant-looking books. And one day he pulled one out and opened it, to take a look. It was the B volume. He opened it in the middle, to a page about birds and how they fly.  The page was composed entirely of diagrams, with short captions to explain them. Not too unlike the comics in the paper that were his main reading material up until then.

Lenny didn't know yet that he had a mind that was interested in and quick to understand how things worked.

He looked for a while at the drawings without making any particular mental effort. Then, in his brain, the drawings converged briefly into a three-dimensional animated model of a bird, complete with the effect of its shape on the movement of air around its body. It was an unusual physical sensation, like a glowing or buzzing, to have this happening inside his head. His head felt, not larger, but as if everything else in there had backed up against the walls to make room for this display. It was interesting. He let it happen for some minutes, then flipped back and forth through the pages to see what else was in there.

When Edie came looking for him, she found him on the floor of his room, sitting in that funny way he had, with his legs forming a w, his round, blond Polish head bent over a picture of some kind printed in color on a clear plastic page. It seemed to be about blood and veins. Yuck, thought Edie. She didn't like being reminded that people had insides.

Lenny looked up with a happy grin.

"What are you doing?" she asked him. She could see what he was doing; what she wanted to know was, why was he doing it?

"Reading," he said. "About how blood gets pumped around our bodies. Look at this picture."

"No thanks," said Edie. "I just ate."

"Is it okay if I read these?" asked Lenny.

"Sure," she said. "As long as you put them back in the right order when you're done." She believed that saying yes should always be accompanied by a condition, or a warning. Or both.

"And don't sit with your legs like that," she said. "You'll get arthritis."

Reading the encyclopedias became one of Lenny's favorite pastimes. He liked playing ball, too, or tag, or riding bikes. But he wasn't that good at throwing or running or balancing. What he really liked was explaining to Debbie and Phil and whoever else was around how if you were way out somewhere in space, the Big Dipper wouldn't look like the Big Dipper at all, because the stars weren't really next to each other, it just looked that way from earth. He did it with tennis balls and golf balls and wiffle balls. He put them all around the yard, on the picnic table and the clothes pole and down on the ground, then made them sit in the one spot, the "earth spot," where the balls formed the Dipper.

He spent hours examining the individual pieces of gravel in the driveway to identify them.

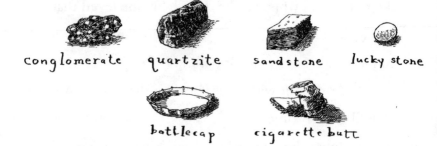

conglomerate   quartzite   sandstone   lucky stone

bottlecap   cigarette butt

He looked at leaves and feathers and bugs through a magnifying glass. Everyone thought he would be a scientist or something brainy.

"How come you know so many things," his mother asked him, "and you don't get better grades?"

Lenny didn't know. He shrugged his shoulders.

"School is boring," he said.

It wasn't exactly what he meant. But it was close.

It was his father, Leon, who went down to the basement one day after work to take a shower and found Lenny sitting on the floor in a jumble of parts, with a screwdriver in his hand. He had taken apart an old vacuum cleaner.

"What do you think you're doing?" Leon asked him. "Put that back together."

He just said it. He didn't really expect Lenny to put it back together. The amazing thing was that Lenny did. Even more amazing, when Lenny flipped the switch, the vacuum cleaner, which hadn't worked for years, roared to life. Leon stared.

"Who showed you how to do that?" asked Leon. "Did you just figure it out yourself?"

"I read about it," said Lenny. "In a book. About small motor repair."

"Same difference," said Leon. "I could look at that book and it would look like Greek to me."

dirt→

mists of time

Leon told everyone about Lenny and the vacuum cleaner. He told everyone when Lenny fixed the toaster, too.

Lenny felt the satisfaction of understanding something in his mind and making it become real with his own hands. Multiplied by the light and warmth of his father's pride. He started fixing things right and left. His metamorphosis from bookworm to gearhead was swift and complete, and he didn't look back.

It could have gone another way. Some perceptive science teacher could have seen past Lenny's shyness and how he was flustered by taking tests. But that didn't happen.

The junior high shop teacher saw his abilities and appreciated them. He steered Lenny toward the vocational-technical track.

Debbie and Phil were sorted into academic, which led to college prep. Everyone assumed that whoever was doing the sorting knew what they were doing. It was all done scientifically, with grades and test scores.

Maybe it was some kind of tragedy that no one spotted who Lenny could be. Or maybe it wasn't. Lenny didn't need someone to tell him who he was. A bird had flown inside his head. He knew how vacuum cleaners worked. And there were a lot of other things he knew.

He had started down a separate path, though, another path than the one his old friends were taking. It was hard to tell how far apart the paths would eventually veer. There were already signs of veering. No one in academic, for example, pinched snuff. Lenny hadn't thought about that before, but he saw it now. He saw that Debbie and Phil had other opinions about it than he did. Phil was hanging out of the passenger side window, and Debbie had her shirt pulled over her nose. Lenny considered this. He was a considerate person.

"All right," he said. He took the wad from his cheek and chucked it at the dirt around his mother's petunias. But although he was stronger now, and more coordinated than he had been as a child, his aim was still lousy. The tobacco hit the side of the house with a wet, brown splat.

"Rats," he said. He looked around for a rag, found an old T-shirt, and got out of the truck to scrub it away before his mother saw it. Debbie and Phil got out, too.

"I need your spit," said Lenny. "Mine's too brown."

They got down on their knees and took turns spitting at the brown stain on the concrete foundation block. In between Lenny rubbed with the old T-shirt until the small brown splat faded and spread to a large pale one that was hardly even noticeable in the spring twilight.

CHAPTER 8

Easy Basin Wrench, or Debbie Has a Mechanical Moment, Too

"Hello!" said Debbie.

"What?" asked her father, from under the kitchen sink.

"Hello!" she said again.

"Hello," he answered.

"That's the first thing it says in the instructions," she said. "Then it says,

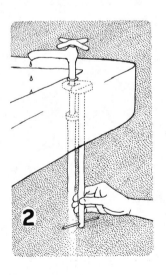

Easy Basin Wrench with more quality and most quantity of every place. And is favored with the patronages of common sense and wisdom. The best for you and friends around the world."

"Does it say anything about how to use it?"

"Let me see. It says, **Precise teeth are biting sharply the slippery oil to a grip.** Does that help?"

"Not yet. Keep going."

"**Jaws seek all position at pivot. The action can then be more skillful. Easily to put or also remove.** Who wrote this?"

"Someone who doesn't speak English," said her dad. He unfurled himself out from under the sink along with the odd-looking tool, and together they studied the instruction sheet. Fortunately, there were also diagrams they could be confused by.

"I like the way it sounds, though," said Debbie. "Listen: **Always care to respect the tool, and it will serve you for indefinite years, even to your children.**"

"That would be you," said her father. "I'll leave it to you in my will."

They decided that Debbie, since she was smaller and more flexible, might be able to maneuver better among the buckets and cleaning products and pipes. After checking the pictures again and examining the mechanism of the basin wrench, she crawled in backward, like a crab. She oriented herself in relation to the pipes.

She put the jaws easily in position.

The precise teeth bit sharply the slippery oil to a grip.

The action was more skillful.

It only took a couple of minutes, and she felt respect, admiration even, for the tool.

Sliding back out, she handed it to her dad. She stood up and washed her hands in the sink while he watched the pipe below to satisfy himself that the dripping had stopped.

It was satisfying. Debbie considered, briefly, becoming a plumber. Showing up at someone's door with the basin wrench, everyone so glad to see her. On the other hand, people would call on the phone in the middle of the night. She would have to get out of her warm bed and go mess with cold, slimy pipes in flooded basements. Wouldn't she? And then there would be all those clogged toilets and drains.

"How about some bean soup?" said her dad. He emptied the can into a pot and mixed it with water while Debbie got out the cheese and crackers and ketchup and poured glasses of milk.

The basin wrench, back in its cardboard sleeve, was stashed under the sink, waiting for another opportunity to serve. It wasn't in a hurry. It was made of heavy cast aluminum and it could wait for indefinite years.

CHAPTER 9

Guitar Lessons

The floor of the church basement was speckled green linoleum. Whitewashed ductwork was suspended from the low ceiling, which was held up at intervals by thick, round pillars made of something. A picture of Jesus suffering little children to come unto Him hung on a paneled wall next to an attendance chart spattered with foil stars. Outside the window, above the upright piano, the legs of passersby occasionally scissored from left to right, or right to left.

Somewhere inside these walls lurked the means to produce spaghetti dinners. Somewhere in the shadowy recesses there could be trays of cookies sprinkled with colored sugar, and cans of Hi-C waiting to blend with ginger ale and become punch in a cut-glass bowl, from whence it could be dipped into water-soluble paper cups. Somewhere there had to be at least some of those pastel mints. At the present moment, though, none of these things was visible. The only aroma in the room was of floor wax.

Hector opened his guitar case and lifted out the guitar. He was the first one there, but there was another guitar case sitting on the floor, and a circle of metal folding chairs, and the lights were on. So he was pretty sure he was in the right place.

A church basement was not where he had imagined learning to play the guitar. Hector had not imagined having the Presbyterian youth minister for his teacher, either. His mother had heard about these lessons, which were free, and his parents said that if he took the free lessons, they would buy him a guitar.

This was the danger of sharing your dreams with your parents. If you told them you wanted to learn to play the guitar, all they heard you say was, "I want to learn to play the guitar," and then they found some practical, convenient, cheap way, often involving a church basement, for you to do it.

But Hector had not come up with any plan of his own. And owning a guitar seemed like an important stepping stone on the way to being a guitar player. So he pawned his soul and said he would take the lessons from the Presbyterian youth minister. What the hell, he thought. Or heck, he thought. What the heck.

Six people with guitars trickled into the church basement, not counting Pastor Don. Two were adults: a gray-haired woman named Mary, and Mr. Schimpf ("Bob"), who had been Hector's pack leader the year he was a Cub Scout. Probably

Mr. Schimpf was looking to be able to play songs around the campfire. Mary had half-spectacles. Hector didn't notice much else about her, because his attention was drawn at that moment to two girls he didn't know who had just come in together.

One girl looked as if she might be Hector's age and one seemed older, maybe Rowanne's age. The older girl told Pastor Don her name was Robin. Hector didn't quite catch the younger one's name. It almost sounded like she said, "Metal," but he didn't think that could be right.

Whatever her name was, she was pretty. She had a thick, careless braid of chestnut hair, a quick smile, and dark, merry eyes. She wore some kind of a fuzzy lavender pullover, and when she crossed her legs and lifted her guitar onto her lap, she had an interesting way of tucking the foot of the bottom leg back under her chair that made Hector feel melty. He looked away in self-preservation.

To Hector's left was

(BACK)   (FRONT)

whose first name was Dan. Many girls at school were infatuated with his shallow athletic splendor and his golden handsome features that were biologically inherited and had nothing to do with the kind of person he might actually be.

Hector wondered what PERSIK 45 was doing there. Wasn't there some sport that needed to be excelled at? He wondered if Metal was the kind of girl who fell in love with football players. He wondered if there was a kind of girl who didn't fall in love with football players. He peeked at her over the rims of his glasses, his face tilted down at his guitar as if he were inspecting it. She was talking to her friend. There was a small brown mole on her cheek, half an inch from the corner of her mouth.

Dan Persik grunted, "Hey," at Hector, acknowledging that he knew him from somewhere, maybe from ten years of being in the same class at school or living on the same block since their respective births.

Hector grunted, "Hey," back, completing the caveman greeting ritual.

To Hector's right sat Russell Kebbesward. A lock of dark hair fell onto his ivory forehead, and his cheeks and his heavy forearms were flushed with rosy feathers of concentration and effort, even before the class started.

To Russell's right were Mary and Mr. Schimpf, then Pastor Don. He was wearing his pastor's outfit, the black shirt with the black and white stand-up collar, and a cardigan sweater.

Pastor Don's orange fuzz of hair was retreating from his pink forehead. His voice was high and fuzzy, too, and on the thin side, but he was not afraid to use it. He launched into a song almost immediately, accompanying himself on the guitar in order to:

a) show them what they, too, would soon be able to do?

b) prove that he knew how to play the guitar?

c) get everyone in the mood?

Hector thought maybe also to

d) perform for an audience. Maybe there had been a time, a moment, when he had made the choice between being a rock star and being a Presbyterian minister. He had that funny voice, but he seemed to enjoy performing. He threw his head back and scrunched his eyes shut and emoted. He did as much as could be done with that voice. The abandoned rock star option had not quite given up. It had not completely faded away.

His guitar playing wasn't fancy, but it worked. When he finally finished his song several minutes later, everyone clapped.

"That was just delightful," said the woman named Mary, setting off a ripple of murmured agreement that swelled, then faded into a pause.

And then they got down to business.

They learned how to tune their guitars, and they learned the G, C, and D chords. They had to strum while switching between chords at unpredictable intervals, in response to Pastor Don's shouted commands. Hector found himself intently focused on the fingers of his left hand.

The sound made by seven beginning guitarists and one more advanced guitarist strumming simultaneously but not in unison in a cavernous church basement was proof that sound is a physical occurrence. You could feel the sound waves colliding. They took up space.

Pastor Don had a strong, steady strum, and there was a definite difference between his G chord and his C chord. He somehow kept his inept band of wild strummers bound loosely together, and even managed to convey the idea that they were moving forward, that what they were doing had something to do with music.

At some point he began singing "You Are My Sunshine," giving the impression that they were actually playing a song. When he switched over to "This Land Is My Land," which apparently they also already knew, Mr. Schimpf joined in, followed by the gray-haired Mary. Their voices flowed in short bursts, ebbing when they had to make chord changes. Russell stopped playing altogether to give his full attention to singing "This Land Is My Land" in his sonorous, melancholy bass. The singing was spreading clockwise around the circle. It had arrived at Hector.

He looked to his left. PERSIK 45 didn't look like he would be singing. He was studiously bent over his guitar, stealing glances at Russell and Pastor Don. Hector saw one of the glances, but he could not read it. There might be derision in it, but there were other possibilities. Maybe PERSIK 45 had a headache, or abdominal discomfort. Or maybe it was a glance of admiration, as expressed by the facial muscles of a football player.

The two girls weren't singing yet, but they didn't

look like they thought singing would be stupid. They were just concentrating on their chords.

Hector could pretend he was concentrating on his chords.

But what the heck, he thought. He started singing. Screw the football player. He liked to sing.

When the class was over, Hector maneuvered himself across the circle and opened his guitar case on the floor next to the two girls. He thought he had pulled this off smoothly, appearing to glance around casually for an empty spot, then heading for this one as if it were the only space available, despite the fact that the cluster of chairs and people and guitars filled only about 3 percent of the large, low room.

"So," he said (very casually) to the younger girl, "what did you say your name was?"

"Meadow," she said.

"Metto?" he repeated, not understanding what she meant.

"You know; butterflies, flowers, bees, grass, sunshine: Meadow."

"Oh. That's a really unusual name."

"Hector's an unusual name, too."

"But it's a name. *Meadow* is, like, a word. It's a really nice word, but it's not usually a name."

"Well, I heard my dad say it would have been more precise to call me *Tent*, but *Meadow* seemed better for a name. I guess they used to go camping a lot. Why did your parents call you Hector? If you're going to be technical, that's a word, too. Why would you name your child a word that means 'to bother people'?"

Most people didn't know that, thought Hector. He said, "That's small *h* hector. Capital *h* Hector was a Trojan, in the Trojan War. But I'm actually named after the leader of a Cuban band that played at a dance where my mom and dad met or got engaged or something."

"Same thing, then," said Meadow. "Sort of."

Hector thought it was going really well, but he

didn't know what else to say. So after hesitating for a moment, he said, "See you next week, then," and turned away. He felt the milk of human kindness go coursing all through him. He felt warmth for all mankind.

He turned toward Russell Kebbesward, who stood next to a folding chair where his loaded guitar case was precariously balanced. Both plump hands were in his pockets with the thumbs hooked outside. His brown, soulful eyes were focused on something that wasn't there, a spot moving in midair. They always looked that way.

"How's it going, Russell?" said Hector.

"Well," said Russell, turning slightly in Hector's direction. "It's going well. Thank you."

It seemed as if Russell might be gathering his thoughts to go on and Hector, feeling so warm and milky and kind, waited.

He set his guitar case back on the floor.

He began to suspect, though, that Russell's thoughts were not gathering at all, that if they even existed, they were wandering through his head like lurching strangers on a moving train. If any two of them met up, it would be purely accidental.

He glanced over his shoulder and saw the rest of the class heading for the exit. Mr. Schimpf was chatting with Mary, Dan Persik was walking out with Meadow and Robin. His head was bent toward them in that big-tall-handsome-football-player-talking-to-pretty-girl way. Their faces were tilted back up at him, but Hector couldn't see them. He could only see their hair, part of their ears, and a sliver of their cheeks. It was possible that they were just listening out of politeness, not enjoyment. It was possible.

He watched as they squeezed through the double doors all at once, in a tight little group with their guitar cases, making a joke of it. Their laughter bounced around the hollow stairwell, multiplying by echoes and spilling back into the room until the doors fell shut. A couple of seconds later three pairs of legs scissored past outside the window above the piano, accompanied by the scraping of feet and a murmur of muffled voices that came, then went.

Hector turned back to Russell. Pastor Don came over, too, making them another threesome.

"We had some fine voices here tonight," he said. "Yours among them."

"Thank you," said Russell.

Again, he looked as if he might say more. Again, he didn't.

To keep things moving, Hector said, "I liked that song you played at the beginning. Is that pretty hard to play?"

But he only half-listened to Pastor Don's response, which was lengthy and enthusiastic. He was probably a nice guy, an interesting guy. He was probably saying something interesting. But an important part of Hector was no longer in the building. What am I doing here? he thought. What do these people have to do with me? Looking from one to the other.

"Well, I've got to go, then," he said. "See you next week." This, for the second time that evening.

As he headed through the double doors, up through the echoing stairwell and outside, he remembered saying it the first time, when he said it to Meadow. What a funny name, he thought. But a pretty name. Beautiful, really. All sunny and "bright golden haze" and all that. It seemed like she ought to have golden hair with that name, but she seemed sunny, anyway.

Hector thought up some similar, corresponding names for himself. Tree. Bark. Fjord. Cliff. Rock. Bam-Bam. Maybe not Bam-Bam. That would be more like Dan Persik. How about Storm? he thought as a sudden powerful gust of sharp air propelled him across the street. How about Rain? Wind? Sprinkle? Monsoon? Wet Pedestrian with Cardboard Guitar Case. Dash. Flash. Trip. Slip. Sprawl. Rip?

He managed, though, to hold the guitar case aloft, like a trophy.

CHAPTER 10
Conversation in the Dark: Brilliant Eskimo Thoughts

P: Do you think things are meant to be?

D: What do you mean?

P: You know, how people say, "It was meant to be," or, "It wasn't meant to be." Or, "they were meant for each other."

D: You mean like (singing) "they say for every boy and girl, there's just one love in this whole world. . . ."

P: Yeah, like that.

D: I don't know. In one way, it makes you think,

"Oh, I don't have to worry, it's all taken care of, it will all work out." But in another way, it's like, what if your life turns out really lousy, is it supposed to make you feel better that somebody planned that for you? And there's nothing you can do about it?

P: I think it does make some people feel better. That's when they say, "God works in mysterious ways." Although no one wants to be the one He's working on that way. It makes people feel like there is some really worthwhile reason that they're having such a crappy life. And like they will be rewarded later.

D: It doesn't make me feel better. I think sometimes things just happen. And also, I think people can make things happen.

P: I wish I could make myself be taller.

D: Taller? Why?

P: I just want to be closer to eye level. I'm tired of talking to people's chests. If I were in a movie, I'd have to stand on a box. I'm like a beautiful person who's been put in a short, pudgy body with frizzy hair.

D: I don't think of you as short. Or pudgy. And I like your hair. Your hair is perfect on you.

P: I don't think of me as being short, either. In fifth grade, I was the tallest girl in the class. I was even taller than the boys. But then I stopped growing and everyone passed me up. I still think I'm tall until I look around.

D: You could wear really big platform shoes.

P: I want to. My mom won't let me buy them. She says I'll fall and break something.

D: They do look kind of tricky. But people wear them. They look more comfortable than high heels—at least your feet aren't tilted at such a steep angle—and they seem less tippy.

P: Miss Epler wears them all the time.

D: She's trying to command authority.

P: She hasn't learned how yet. She still acts like a human being.

D: What if someone gave you platform shoes as

a gift? Would your mom let you wear them?

P: Who's going to give me platform shoes as a gift? You?

?: Have you ever noticed that if there's a character in a movie who's supposed to be not-beautiful, they just take an incredibly beautiful person and do something to her hair and make her wear big, thick glasses?

?: And wrinkled, baggy clothing.

?: And then sometime during the movie, she realizes she really doesn't need glasses after all and she puts on some nice clothes and combs her hair and all her problems are solved. Unless it's a sad movie and she dies.

?: Or she finds out she really does have to wear glasses.

?: That would be really sad.

?: That would be too sad. I don't think I could watch a movie that sad.

?: It does help to wear nice clothes and comb your hair, though.

?: Then you can be a neat ugly person.

❦

?: I like Miss Epler. She's so different from other people in Seldem and Birdvale.

?: I want to be different from people in Seldem and Birdvale, too. I wonder how you get that way.

?: You have to come from somewhere else.

?: Oh. Is that the only way? Couldn't you *go* somewhere else?

?: Then you'd still be like someone from Seldem, but maybe nobody there would know what that was.

?: Because for them, you'd be from Somewhere Else.

?: I guess so. I guess that would work.

❦

?: Have you ever been somewhere, and it hit you that if you lived there instead of where you do, your whole life might be really different?

?: It probably wouldn't be that different, if you're still the same person.

?: I think it could. I think if you wear different socks, your whole life can be different. It's like that thing of, if a butterfly flaps its wings in Indonesia, it can cause a tidal wave in Florida. Or maybe it's Africa, I forget. But that's not really what I was thinking about. It was more like, if Albert Einstein had grown up in, maybe an Eskimo village, would he still have been brilliant?

?: He would have had brilliant Eskimo thoughts. He would still have done something amazing with, like, blubber and ice, but maybe we wouldn't all know about it. I think it makes more difference where you are if you're not Albert Einstein. I mean, more difference to you. To the world, it probably makes more difference where Albert Einstein is.

☙❧

?: Do you think that Dan Persik might like me?

?: Why would you want him to?

?: His locker is next to mine, and he always says "Hi" to me in a really nice way, it's like a teasing way, and then I get all stupid and I don't know what to say back, besides, "Hi."

P: That seems like an okay thing to say back.

D: But I want to say something more. I mean, do you think—

P: No.

D: Why not?

P: It wasn't meant to be.

CHAPTER 11
Hector's First Song

It was just the refrain, and it was actually more spoken than sung, but it had a universal theme and a good beat. You could dance to it. It went like this:

I'm thinkin' 'bout,
talkin' 'bout
boys, boys, boys,
I'm talkin' 'bout
girls, girls, girls
(two, three, four)

◖◗

The first part would be sung by a female voice, the second by a male; that's how Hector heard it in his head. It was kind of a Motown thing. He only needed the three chords they had already learned.

But he might need more chords once he thought up some verses.

CHAPTER 12

Truck Lessons

One Saturday only Debbie and Lenny showed up. They were both early, and they sat in companionable silence waiting for the others.

"Where's Phil?" asked Debbie, after thirty seconds or ten minutes, she wasn't sure which.

"At a wedding reception," said Lenny. "His cousin Carol got married today." A few minutes passed, then he asked, "Is Patty coming?"

"No," said Debbie. "It's her great-grandma's ninetieth birthday."

"Wow," said Lenny. "That's pretty old."

"I know," said Debbie. "Really old."

A few more minutes or half an hour passed. Then they both started to speak at once, and what each of them had been about to say was "I wonder where Hector is."

They laughed, then Debbie said that Hector could be anywhere, and they laughed about that. There was a pause, then they both chuckled as if they were still thinking about Hector and where he might be.

Finally Lenny turned the key, and the radio became the third person, filling up the middle section of the wide, blue, vinyl seat. Debbie and Lenny each leaned up against their doors to make room.

It was a pretty good episode, with some new stuff and some that they had heard before. The hour went by.

"Crisscross," said the old movie voice, and then there was the sound of the train wreck.

Lenny turned the key to the completely off position. The other keys on the ring slid down with a slight ching. Probably they always made that ching, but normally it would have been swallowed up in the sounds of conversation. Now it was all by itself:

ching

Debbie found herself wishing that one of the others was there. Or that some other sound would puncture the quiet before it grew too large. The quiet had come out of nowhere; it surprised Lenny, too. Their heads were suddenly empty of the usual easy conversations, their eyes looked through the windshield into the backyards, touching on all the familiar objects, none of which were doing anything worth commenting on, none of them were doing anything at all. Everything was just sitting there.

Some birds began chirping, but it wasn't enough.

They were alone, no one at all was around. He

was a boy and she was a girl. Debbie was thinking she might go home and see what was on TV.

Then without exactly knowing why, Lenny did what any (red-blooded? American?) boy would do. He asked her if she wanted to learn how to drive the truck.

It was an idea that had never been in even the same neighborhood as Debbie's mind. It took her by surprise, so that while her instincts told her the right answer would be "No," they couldn't think right away of why not.

"Are you kidding?" she said. "What if I wrecked it?" This seemed like a pretty obvious reason why not.

"We'll just go back and forth in the driveway," said Lenny. "First and reverse."

"I bet I could still wreck it," said Debbie. She was sticking to this while she waited for reinforcement reasons to arrive.

"You won't wreck it," said Lenny. "I'll show you how. It's not that hard."

He had been surprised by the idea, too, at first,

but it was making a lot of sense to him now. It was something he knew how to do. And it was fun. He didn't know why he hadn't thought of it sooner.

"Your dad doesn't want me driving his truck," said Debbie. She was pretty sure about that.

"He won't care," said Lenny. "But I'll ask him." He got out of the truck, walked over to the screen door, and called in, "Hey Dad, is it okay if I teach Debbie to drive the truck, just in the driveway?" He put his ear to the screen door.

"Hold on," he said over his shoulder, "he must be watching TV." He went inside. A minute later he reappeared.

"It's okay," he told her. "My dad said as long as we stay in the driveway."

The pickup had a stick shift. That's what was so hard to resist. The Pelbry family always had automatics. A stick shift seemed . . . adventurous. And exotic. Europeans and cowboys (well, at least the ones in Marlboro commercials) and race car drivers (she thought) used stick shifts. Her cousin

Dick drove a car with a stick shift, a little sports car with a convertible top.

And it might be an emergency life skill a person should have, along with knowing how to be a waitress or how to resuscitate someone who has been dragged out of a river or a lake. Say, for example, you were riding in a car, a car with a stick shift, and the driver had a heart attack in the middle of nowhere. It would be irresponsible not to know how to drive to a hospital. Especially when someone had offered you the chance to learn.

Maybe she should do it, learn to use the stick shift. If she didn't, she might be sorry someday when a situation like that came up.

"Are you sure your dad said it was okay?" she asked.

"Oh, yeah," said Lenny. "He said it was a good idea."

This wasn't exactly a fib, he thought. It was more like a loose interpretation of something his dad often said while driving, which was "If God hadn't meant

people to fly, he wouldn't have invented Chevys."
He glanced at the clock on the dashboard.

"We have to do it now, though, because he said
he needs the truck in about an hour."

So he taught her to drive the truck. Not everything,
just first gear and reverse. If she were in the
emergency situation with the heart attack–stricken
driver now, she could take him slowly, very slowly
(forward or backward) to the hospital. With any luck,
it wouldn't be very far away and she could get there
by going in a straight line. The picture in her mind
was of a desert scenario, with no large objects
between her and her destination.

Lenny was a good teacher. First he sat in the
driver's seat, showing her how it was done, the clutch
pedal and the gas pedal going up and down like
opposite ends of a seesaw. He was good at explaining
it. He understood how things worked, and he made
it seem simple, so that when Debbie slid across the
seat and behind the wheel, the truck didn't seem

any more mysterious than her mother's sewing machine, which was also operated with a pedal. A large sewing machine moving back and forth in the gravel driveway.

Lenny had demonstrated what would happen if she gave it too much gas or not enough, or let the clutch out too quickly, so Debbie was prepared and didn't panic. She just tried again and again, and after a while she started to get it. She was driving a truck. With a stick shift. She loved it. She loved the knob with the diagram on it and the molded rubber thing that covered up whatever was really happening at the bottom of the stick, something that you couldn't see, you just had to picture it in your mind. She loved balancing the movements of the two pedals, up and down, just so.

Lenny kept his hand on the steering wheel, just in case. This was probably a good thing, because Debbie was feeling the urge to turn it. And to go a little faster. She looked over at Lenny. She was lit up from inside. Her mouth was only in a half smile, but the whole rest of her face looked like it was laughing. Lenny had seen her look that way before. She had looked that way most of their childhood, digging up dirt or playing kickball or tearing around on the bikes. But he hadn't seen her look that way lately.

"This is great," she said. "I want to go somewhere."

Lenny's face was smiling, too. For a minute they were both ten years old. Time travel in real life.

Lenny's fourteen-year-old self, who was keeping an eye on the clock on the dashboard, said, "We can do that next time. My dad needs to use the truck in a couple minutes." He didn't know how that "next time" bit could happen, but he wanted to say it. So he did.

A fact, a feather of knowledge, had been floating around the outside of Debbie's mind searching for a place to enter, for an opening in the light but unbroken cloud cover that had surrounded it a little while ago. As the clouds began to break up and drift apart, it found a current of air and drifted in. She was glad she had kept it out for a while.

"You know," she said, "I was just thinking. I know your dad said it was okay, and all we did was go back and forth in the driveway, but I think my mother—"

"I won't say anything," said Lenny.

"Do you think your dad might mention it to her?"

"I can tell him not to, if you want," said Lenny. Not strictly a fib. He didn't say he *would*.

"Okay," said Debbie. "Thanks. You know my mom." She wasn't her ten-year-old self now, but traces of that self lingered behind, little flecks of joy visible somehow on her eyebrow, and her chin.

"Well," she said. "I better go. See you."

"See you later," said Lenny. He watched her go, then slid back over behind the steering wheel, where the seat was still warm. He flipped the key in the ignition again and moved the radio dial back and forth. He listened to a couple of songs without really paying attention. In the rearview mirror he saw his parents' car pull up the driveway behind him. The tires grumbled over the gravel, the car doors clinked open and thunked shut, their voices, in the middle of some conversation, grew louder as they approached, then stopped.

"Were you just sitting in there by yourself the whole time we were gone?" asked his dad.

"Nope," said Lenny. "Debbie came over for a while to listen to the show."

"Oh. Good," said his dad. "That's nice. Don't sit out here all night, all right? You'll run down my battery."

"I won't," said Lenny.

His parents went inside. He turned the radio off and sat there for a little while longer, watching the backyard dissolve into darkness. And then he went inside, too.

CHAPTER 13

Ravine

The people singing the song were from California. Hector lay peacefully on his back on his carpeted bedroom floor, letting the music from his radio wash over him. His idea had been to do some sit-ups, but once he got down there, it seemed to make more sense to just lie still and gaze up at the ceiling. That's where he was when the song came on the radio. It was a song he liked, and he had heard it many times before. It was the Mamas and the Papas.

They were singing that words of love so soft and tender wouldn't win a girl's heart anymore. And that if you loved her you should ("must") send her somewhere she had never been before.

It was a metaphor. Hector knew that. He didn't think they meant that you were supposed to put the girl on an airplane or something. Still, he thought, to take a girl to a new place, to show her something she hadn't seen. It sounded like a good idea.

Although he wished he were in California, where there were giant redwood trees and Hollywood and canyons and the Pacific Ocean. There were probably a lot of incredible places and things out there that you could show someone for the first time. He tried to think which places you would show someone in Seldem.

As he thought about it Hector realized that, at least at first, the places should be within a fairly short walking distance from guitar lessons. The only places that came to mind immediately were the Tastee-Freez and the gas station. The Tastee-Freez was a good place to go, it was one of his favorite places to go, but he would bet five dollars that Meadow had already been there.

He was going to have to do some research. Using his powerful, well-rested abdominal muscles, he curled to a sitting position and reached for his sneakers.

He started out certain that he would come across any number of interesting spots that had somehow slipped his mind. He had lived here all his life without being bored; he must have been doing or looking at something. But much of what he himself found interesting didn't seem to have the magnitude or kind of interestingness required to be destinations you would invite someone to go see.

He tried to imagine saying, "Do you want to go see this really interesting pile of dirt with pipes sticking out of it?"

Or, "Have you ever been at a used car lot at sunset, when they turn on the string of lightbulbs?"

There was a picturesque old nun who lived in the

old convent by our Lady of Victory. She was a retired nun with a lot of free time on her hands. He had seen her many times, often involved in some unlikely activity that seemed incongruous with her long, flowing, black and white habit. He saw her once clutching a bunch of daffodils in one hand and a ski pole, which she was using as a cane, in the other. Once she was twirling a child's silvery baton with plastic tassels. Today she was pushing a shopping cart full of watermelons down the sidewalk.

But even if you could imagine yourself saying to a girl, "Hey, wanna go see what the old nun is doing tonight?" and even if she were out doing something picturesque, he didn't see how it would lead to holding hands or kissing or anything. There were a lot of things like that.

He was looking for something with immediately apparent beauty or interest, like a waterfall or a mountain or a skyscraper. Even a small one.

"Just one thing," he said to himself. "Just one thing I could show her."

He was about to give up when he noticed the ravine. There was a ravine, falling away behind a chain-link fence. The fence was almost invisible within the complicated weaving of wild vines, saplings, and weeds growing in and out of it. Hector leaned on it and looked over. Two steep banks of tangled lushness, dappled by sunlight sifting through honey locust trees, plunged in rough symmetry down to a merry brook, complete with stepping stones. About twenty-five or thirty feet along, the brook channeled into a concrete culvert under the access road to the Westinghouse plant. As he stood looking, a trailer truck barreled over the culvert. A small, furry animal stood erect before diving out of sight.

Hector took a step back and surveyed the fence for a point of entry. The fence continued almost to the access road, where there was a narrow opening before the beginning of a low wall that kept trucks from sliding off the road and into the ditch. Or rather, the ravine. Passing through the opening, he saw that others had come before him. No one was here now, but a path had been worn, and when he reached the bottom he found charred pieces of wood, cigarette butts, and empty and broken whiskey bottles. And some other trash. A potato chip bag. A shoe. A plastic cigarette lighter. A comb.

Combs, Hector had noticed, were everywhere. Not here, but when you were walking down the street. They were usually the short, black, plastic kind, as if that kind was especially hard to keep imprisoned in a back pocket or a purse. You could sort of picture them, springing silently out of pockets and purses all over town. All over the world. *Boing, boing, boing.* Free! All over the world, hands digging into pockets and purses, searching. But it was too late. They were gone.

He was thinking now that it might not be a good idea to bring Meadow here if it was, like, a drinking spot. For one thing, he didn't know whose drinking spot it was, or how often it was used. He felt a sudden sensation, as if maybe he wasn't alone, as if maybe someone was there right now. He looked, at first just moving his eyes. Then turning around, slowly. But no one was there. He couldn't see anyone.

It was such a pretty little place. The furry creature reappeared from the brook and scampered calmly along the bank. Hector didn't know what it was, but he didn't think it was a rat. He didn't think rats could swim. The Pied Piper and all that.

He squatted down and started filling the potato chip bag with broken glass and whatever else would fit. The shoe was not going to fit into the bag. He considered some of the circumstances under which a person might lose one shoe without noticing it was missing.

The trash looked old. It wasn't fresh trash. He thought he would clean it up and check back, and if fresh trash didn't appear, maybe it would mean that no one came here anymore and it could be his spot. He thought that until a car rumbled by and a paper grocery bag sailed through the foliage just inches from his head. It landed with a thunk and a rip and released its contents at the water's edge. Someone's kitchen garbage. Eggshells and coffee grounds, pork chop bones, a ketchup bottle, some cans and plastic, some greasy paper towels . . .

A breeze stirred the whispering honey locusts, lifted a few wadded-up Kleenexes from the heap, nudged them into the brook. Gently down the stream. Merrily, merrily, merrily. The furry thing was watching, too. Hector felt a kinship with the furry thing. As the so-called higher life form, he felt compelled to remove his fellow-human's garbage from the furry thing's home. It occurred to him that the furry thing might like one or two things in the bag. But he wasn't going to pick through it to find them.

He turned the bag so that the rip was on top and balanced the chip bag full of broken glass on top of that, then carefully stood up and turned. He made his way up the steep path, hoping his unstable parcel of mold, rot, shards, and contagion would not fall apart all over him.

Because his burden of garbage was large and precarious, he could not look down at the path and had to go by the feel of the dirt under his sneakers. He also had to go sideways so he would remain vertical, i.e., not tip over backward. Brambles clawed at his shirttail. Sour aromas filled his nose and swarmed over his skin and clothing. A small jar (olives?) worked itself loose and bounced back down to the bottom.

"I'm sorry," said Hector. "I can't come back for you. I would if I could, but I can't."

At the top he maneuvered backward between the fence and the bridge wall with luck and grace, and he emerged onto the sidewalk with a feeling of triumph, of savoir faire. Until he realized he didn't know what to do next. And that there wasn't a lot of time to think about it. The paper bag was damp. From damp to soggy was a short distance, and from soggy to not even there was even shorter. He strode purposefully toward the center of town, keeping an eye peeled for a garbage can. Something sloshed with each step—he could feel a wetness on his midriff—but he walked on. It was remarkable how under-garbage-canned this area of town was. Also, how much traffic whizzed by, and how so many people stared from their car windows at someone walking down a sidewalk. He tried to maintain a jaunty, nonchalant air as he walked on. A slight ache began to spread through his arms because he could not alter their awkward position.

Hector was within two blocks of the gas station and the blessed garbage can that he knew was there when he felt the paper bag separate into two sections. It was a slight but significant movement. He spread his fingers and tried to increase the viselike grip of his biceps and forearms. He clamped his chin down and shifted into a very fast shuffling walk that had no ups and downs to it, just a smooth forward glide. He moved fluidly in the direction of the garbage can. His whole being was focused on the thought of the can. It was when he reached the edge of the gas station's property line that he came into view of the can itself and saw, remembered, that it had a top on it, a rounded top with a little swinging door, a door too small for his explosive bundle. He wouldn't be able to lift it off without letting go. The garbage can was just outside the door, though, and the door was opening. Someone was coming out. Hector shouted.

"Help!" he yelled as loudly as he could without

moving his chin. "Take the lid off the garbage can! I'm going to explode!"

The person looked at him quizzically, then grasped the situation and pulled at the lid, though the lid was heavy and grimy and it was clear that the person didn't want to do it. The lid came up, the heavy load fell in, and Hector experienced an exquisite relief. His arms tingled with renewed circulation. His legs straightened and his major muscle groups spasmed quietly back to their usual configurations. He felt light and free and happy. Then he felt wet and smelly and stupid.

"What are you doing?" said the person who had helped him. Who was his sister, Rowanne.

"So you were going to take this girl to a drainage ditch?" said Rowanne.

"It's a ravine," said Hector. "It's more like a ravine than a drainage ditch. It's a really pretty spot. Except for the garbage. I don't think it's gonna work. I don't know where else to go, though."

"Why don't you just come here?" asked
Rowanne. They were sitting on a bench at the
Tastee-Freez, eating ice cream cones.

"I mean, for starters," she said. "Then you could
work your way up to the drainage ditch."

Hector licked his cone, considering. He was a
licker. Rowanne was a biter. She was halfway done
and he had barely made a dent.

"You could sit on this bench," she said, "and look
at the view."

"What view?" said Hector. The bench looked out
over the A&P parking lot. Also in sight were the used
car lot, the gas station, and the Idle Hour Restaurant,
with its bobbing neon chicken advertising "Chicken
in the Rough." That meant you ate it out of a plastic
basket lined with wax paper instead of from a dish.
They were in the heart, though not quite the
entirety, of Seldem's commercial district.

"The chicken sign is pretty cool," said Rowanne.

"I like it when the lights come on in the car lot,"
said Hector.

"Oh, so do I," said Rowanne.

"Bring her here," she said. "It's a good place to start. And then I'll try to help you think of something else."

"I'll try, I guess," said Hector. "Ice cream is always good."

"Ice cream is good," said Rowanne. "Ice cream is always good."

The plum tree blossoms,
the new yearbook is opened.
Is that who I am?

CHAPTER 14
Japanese chapter

Debbie and Patty sat in a wooden gazebo. The flowering plums outside were covered with blossoms, as if a giant bowl of popcorn had spilled from the sky, which was blue, and landed in the branches. They were looking at the senior pages of the new yearbooks.

The seniors could have their pictures taken in different settings—leaning against a tree, by a fireplace, wherever they wanted—and they could wear whatever they wanted. A tuxedo, a football uniform, a leather jacket. A beautiful evening gown. A T-shirt and jeans. They could use props: a motorcycle, a guitar, a rose.

A committee of students had chosen a quote, from literature or history, to accompany each person's photograph in the yearbook. They picked them from a book of quotations that was divided into categories like Music, Art, Sports, Intelligence, Friendship, Beauty, Sincerity, Humor, Courage. There were even literature-y ways of saying Headed for Trouble.

You had to wonder how some people felt when they saw the quotes that had been chosen for them:

"Strength lies not in defense but in attack."

—Hitler

This was because he was an offensive lineman on the football team.

"But still," said Debbie. "Hitler?"

Or

"He is happiest of whom the world says least,
      good or bad." —Jefferson

and

      "A nice, unparticular man." —Hardy

"You can tell they didn't know what to say about him," said Patty.

"I think they should do haikus," said Debbie. Maybe because of the gazebo and the plum blossoms and the sparkling water. "Then it can be about nothing but sound like it's about something. Like

      The page is empty.
      Who knows what mystery will
      be written there?"

"It still sounds like there's nothing to say about him."

"*Empty* isn't a good word. It should be more like, 'The page is waiting.'

The page is waiting.

Will anything be written?

It waits and it waits."

"The page gets bored and falls asleep."

"Go to our class."

"Okay. Here."

"Is that how I look?"

"No." "But it's a photograph."

"That doesn't matter."

"Jeff White is handsome,

but his hair is so greasy.

If he would wash it—"

"Look, here's Dan Persik . . .

I could look at him all day."

"Too bad he's a jerk."

"He has hidden depths."
"You think that about everyone." "Because it's true.

                  "Like Sara Stavor.
                        She seems kind of boring, but
                        then she makes you laugh."

            "What about Pam Burke?
               She doesn't have hidden depths."
            "Her depths are shallow.

She has hidden shallows."
      They fell silent, perusing the familiar faces:

                        all those necklaces and bracelets,
                        she jingles
When I think of him,
I feel sorry for him, but
look: he looks happy.

                  roly-poly, but graceful, how does she do that?

maybe he's brilliant
sometimes friendly and funny
sometimes sarcastic
you have to check his mood before speaking
like putting your head out the door to see how cold

That sleepover in sixth grade.
The dance when she

The thoughts were that quick. But each thought could hold a story. Like

I went to a sleepover at her house when we were in sixth grade. Somehow I was cooler then, I think. (What happened?) Other people were there—it was a pajama party—but I was the chosen friend of the evening. I don't know why.

She said, "Come with me while I shave my legs." We went into the bathroom and I sat on the edge of the tub while she shaved her legs with an electric razor.

"I have to shave them every other night," she said. Wow, I thought. I had never shaved my legs at all and felt suddenly how golden and furry they were, like a bumblebee.

I was wearing shortie pajamas that were my favorites, but now I wished that they were long ones, or a nightgown. Or one of those exercise tents that your whole body fits inside so you can sweat.

She looked so elegant, shaving her long, tanned legs. Expertly. You could tell that she really did do it a lot.

Later on, a year or so, we went to one of the dances together. There was a boy there, older, who liked her. She was so pretty, and she looked older, too. Mature or sophisticated or something. They danced together a lot.

When they sat down on the bleachers, I went over and sat down, too. I mean, we came together, and they were just sitting there.

She turned and looked at me and it might have been pity or it might have had an apology in it, but it was definitely Get Lost. Don't be a child.

I sat there for a few seconds more, looking into the dark room full of people dancing while she and her guy gazed into each other's eyes and palpated each other's hands. Then I said, "Well, see you later." I went to the girls room and looked at myself in the mirror. I thought I still looked okay. I came back into the gym through a door toward the back where it was really dark, and climbed up to the top *row of the bleachers. I felt ten years old and a thousand years old, but I didn't know how to be my own age. I had never felt that way before, but now I feel like that a lot.*

Later, while we waited for our ride, she acted like nothing had happened. But it had.

That sleepover in sixth grade. The dance when she

That quick.
Other faces had other stories.

Out of the cocoon,
something new: is this one still
a caterpillar?

With the sleep-over, the dance in her head, Debbie looked at her own picture and saw a caterpillar.

The sparkling water, purple concrete elephant: Seldem Pool & Patio.

When Patty looked at it, she only saw her friend. Her gaze bounced over to Lenny's picture, and she smiled as she remembered how just that day in science class, Mrs. Lewandowski had asked her to find a place to plug in the overhead projector. All the visible outlets were full, so she had crawled under a table on her hands and knees. When she came out, Lenny was standing there.

"What are you doing?" he asked.

"Looking for an outlet," she said.

Lenny said, "Have you tried tennis?"

She looked up from the yearbook to tell Debbie about it, but Debbie spoke first.

"Look, there goes Hector."
"I wonder why he's running."
"His bag is breaking."

The bag was a grocery bag, but the items escaping from it—crumpled tissues, bent cans—looked like used groceries, also known as garbage. Why was Hector running down the street in this part of town with a bag of garbage?

His shirttails flew out behind him. He was too far away to call out to, over the traffic noise. It was interesting, Debbie thought, how you could recognize a person, even from a distance, and even when you couldn't see the person's face. Even when the person was scuttling along the sidewalk like a crustacean. What was it, exactly, that you recognized?

In Hector's case, it was probably his hair. But there was something else, too, she thought. Something so Hector-y about his whole self. She watched him for a moment, wondering what it was that gave him away. She wondered if she had something like that.

CHAPTER 15

Guitar Progress

It wasn't that hard to make one beautiful sound on the guitar. The easiest thing in the world was to hold down the two strings for the E minor chord and draw your thumb across all six strings, down below. A really beautiful sound. Melancholy, but satisfying.

Hector was developing callouses on his fingertips, which was good. He could play some songs and sing them at the same time. "This Land Is Your Land," "Greensleeves," a few others.

Sometimes he felt fine about where he was. And sometimes it seemed that there was no road that led from the church basement guitar class to where he wanted to go. Sometimes he couldn't even remember where that was, or why he had wanted to go there.

But he had gotten into the habit of going into his room and picking up the guitar. And once he picked it up, he did all the things he knew how to do, then messed around a little bit. A lot, sometimes.

CHAPTER 16
Home Work

Lenny dropped his books on the bed and picked up a magazine. The creak of floorboards in his parents' bedroom told him that his father was awake. Leon was on third shift, sleeping all day with the curtains drawn and waking up in mid-afternoon to the aromas of the beginnings of dinner: onions and celery softening in melted butter. It wasn't a bad way to wake up. There was still some afternoon and a full evening ahead.

Working day shift, you got home around this same time, but you could be too tired to enjoy it. That was just his opinion. Leon opened his bedroom door and walked the two steps to Lenny's open doorway.

"Good morning," he said. The afternoon light was dim and indirect on this side of the house, but it was enough to make him squint as his eyes adjusted. The movement of squinting triggered the tumbling down of a few more locks of dark hair onto his forehead.

"Good morning," said Lenny. He had to grin at his dad's face, unshaven and puffy with sleep, eyelids hunched together to keep out the brightness that wasn't even bright.

"You didn't get enough beauty sleep," he said. "You better go back to bed."

"I don't think it would do any good," said his dad. "Listen, we have some time before dinner, can you give me a hand getting that old washing machine out of the cellar? There's a guy at work who wants it. He fixes them up and sells them."

"Sure," said Lenny.

They went down into the basement, which was more of a solid than a space. It was a Chinese puzzle made out of a haphazard accumulation of snow tires, lawn chairs, suitcases, cases of unreturned pop and beer bottles, picnic coolers, furniture and boxes of dishes from Lenny's grandmother's house that Edie didn't like but Leon couldn't bear to get rid of, along with boxes no one had even peeked in for years. Who knew what all was in there? The washing machine was roughly in the center of the whole mess, its shiny, rounded surface glinting out from under a couple of rolled-up carpets and clothesline props. Extricating it without causing the entire arrangement to collapse would be like pulling out the middle pickup stick. A really heavy pickup stick. Lenny and Leon studied the situation.

"We should get rid of some of this stuff. Clean this place up," said Leon.

"You think so?" said Lenny.

"We could make a nice TV room down here," said Leon.

"Yup," said Lenny. He didn't bother thinking about this idea; he had heard it before and he knew it wasn't going to happen. "I think I can climb up and roll those carpets back a little and push the dresser sideways a couple inches, turn the bikes so they're straight. Then we only have to move the boxes in front out of the way and we can drag the washer right out."

"Let's give it a try," said his dad.

Leon was strong, and Lenny was starting to get strong, too. Together they hefted the washing machine up the narrow cellar steps, one at a time.

"Does anyone still even use this kind?" asked Lenny, during a pause. It was a wringer washer, with rollers.

"I guess someone does," said Leon. "I told him what it was, and he said he'd give me twenty bucks for it. I figured it was worth it just to get it out of here."

They banged out through the screen door and set the heavy monster down on the stoop before the final heave and shuffle over the gravel and up onto the bed of the pickup. With a final grating screech, they shoved it toward the cab, then secured it with a complex arrangement of rope.

"Success," said Lenny.

Through her open window, Debbie could hear their voices and all the banging, shuffling, and scraping noise, but none of it registered. She was doing homework, and she was absorbed in thought.

She didn't know his middle name—that could be the tiebreaker. She was doing FLAME with her name and Dan Persik's name, where you write down your names, cross off the letters that are in both, then count the letters that are left and see where it takes you on the word FLAME. For example:

~~D~~EBBIE

~~D~~AN

leaves seven letters.

FLAME

12345

67

L stands for Lovers. However,

~~DEBRA~~

~~DANIE~~L

leaves only five letters, and *E* stands for Enemies. DAN PERSIK and DEBBIE PELBRY was *E* for Enemies, while DANIEL PERSIK and DEBRA PELBRY was another *L*. The forms had to match: both just first names, both full names and so on. The other letters stood for Friends, Affectionate, and Married. So there was a pretty good chance of something good.

It was funny that they had the same initials. In fact, Dan Persik's locker was right next to hers because of alphabetical order: Pelbry, Persik. It seemed like that could mean something. Or not. She decided to try "Deb" and "Dan." No one called her Deb. But it was a legal nickname for Debra. She tried it.

D̶EB
D̶AN
4: *M!*

Not that she believed in it. She removed the page from her spiral notebook, folded it in half, put it in the desk drawer under some pencils, and whipped through some quadratic equations (she didn't exactly get what they were for, but she could solve them). Then she described her favorite meal in three paragraphs of German while scraps of the day floated randomly in and out of her head.

The scrap that kept popping up was the one where Dan Persik said hi to her.

"Debbie Pelbry," he had said. "Hello, there."

He said it when she was standing in front of her open locker in her bunny-free jeans. That were the right length. But he had caught her unaware. Sometimes that was good—it meant you didn't have time to freeze up, and you could behave like a normal person and have a natural response. And then sometimes it meant you looked startled, like a bunny at a loud noise. Like a bunny at any noise. That was sort of natural, too, in a way, and could have a certain kind of charm, she thought. She hoped.

"Oh," she said involuntarily. Startled bunny response. Then, "Hi!" Her mind dissolving into a rosy, patchy fog that drifted to the skin on her face, leaving a vacancy in her head. Something else. She needed to say something else. What? What?

"How's it going?"

Dan Persik said it. Just when Debbie thought of saying it, he said it, and now she needed to come up with another idea.

He said it in a friendly way. Almost flirting. He talked that way to everyone. Even so, it was pretty irresistible. What should she say back, though? Something funny. Something friendly and funny and light and also irresistible. But soon. Time was passing. Seconds, eons were slipping by.

Dan Persik had paused, looking at Debbie, waiting for her to answer. She had to say something.

"Fine," she said. "It's going fine." Oh, barf.

"Good," he said. "That's good." He smiled at her. It was a really nice smile, and something about it made her laugh, just a little bit.

"What's so funny?" he asked. With curiosity.

"I don't know," she said. "Nothing." She really

didn't know, but a couple of times during the day they passed in the hall, and he looked at her and said, "What's so funny?" Each time, she smiled involuntarily, blushed, and said, "Nothing. Nothing is funny."

It wasn't much, she knew that. But it felt like something to her. She couldn't help thinking about it, about Dan Persik and his smile. As she read her science assignment, the brief exchange took on the proportions of a TV miniseries, appearing in a variety of settings and situations.

"What's so funny?" he would say to her, with his irresistible, curious, interested smile as they walked down the hall together at school. As they sat on their beach towels on the grass at the pool at Bouquet Park. As they wandered through the golden green fields of the brief Siberian summer. (As in the old version of *Dr. Zhivago*, recently on TV.)

"I don't know," she would say, smiling enigmatically. "Nothing." Pushing a sun-bleached strand of hair behind her ear, like Julie Christie.

He wasn't really a donkey.

Dan Persik was under a spell, conferred by a magic jersey and a powerful potion of lucky genes and emerging hormones. The spell gave him special powers. He was having a lot of fun with it. Who wouldn't?

He was untroubled, which made him even more appealing.

It was a time-sensitive spell, with a catch. He didn't know that yet. Here was the deal: He had to somehow learn certain lessons, involving humility, compassion, respect, and independent thinking. Math and verbal skills would also be useful. Actually, these are the same lessons everyone has to learn, but part of the spell was a blinder effect that made it a lot more difficult.

It could take five minutes or five years or forever. It wasn't clear how it was supposed to happen. Probably through encountering certain significant persons, like maybe a sick person, an old person, a dead person, and a monk in a yellow robe. A white rabbit, a hookah-smoking caterpillar, and a walking deck of cards. Or it could be a lonely misfit, a shy girl and . . . a wrinkled crone bearing magic pieces of fruit? It could be almost any combination of people or events. The key was, something had to penetrate his golden aura and touch his soul.

If he learned these lessons, he would get to keep some of the special powers, though they would matter less because he would have some new ones.

If he didn't learn them, he would remain a large, furry, willfully stupid animal.

If he learned just some of them, he would be somewhere in between, but any would be better than none.

The likelihood of any one result was completely unpredictable.

In the meantime, he had to maintain a "C" average to stay on the team. It wasn't that difficult. He wrote his name and the date at the top of the paper, all in capitals, with a sharp, slashing slant.

The house was empty when Hector took out his guitar, and he left his bedroom door wide open. He opened the notebook on his desk to the back and flipped forward a few pages until he found his newest song. The new idea he was trying with this song was that, since he wasn't good enough at finger picking to do it and sing at the same time, he was going to strum while he sang, and in between verses he would do the finger picking. Besides the fact that it was the only way he could do it so far, it seemed like that's when people would notice it more, anyway.

He thought the refrain of the song was really a good one. Basically, he just wanted to sing the refrain over and over, but he knew you had to break it up with some verses, so he was working on that.

Here's how the refrain went:

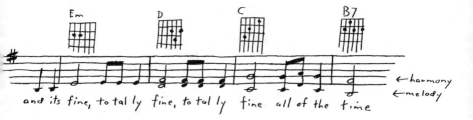

It sounded so good he hoped someone hadn't already written it—that could happen. How would you know?

What was brilliant, Hector felt, was that the words said "fine, totally fine" and so on, but it had this minor-key sound so you were left thinking, well, is it fine, or maybe it isn't?

He didn't have the verses, or a tune for the verses, yet, but he had a feeling about them. A bittersweet feeling. The verses should be about things that weren't really fine at all, but—or maybe there should be a verse or two about things that really were fine.

He couldn't decide if it should be about social injustice or about the human condition or about love. Maybe all of them. Maybe one verse each. You could have the same reaction to each one. You could say the same words with different feelings:

and it's fine, totally fine, totally fine, all of the time.

It could be dark, bitter, ironic.

Or it could be light, joyful, carefree.

Pick a feeling, you could feel it when you sang these words. It could be a song about . . .

Something Hector had heard a day or so ago came back to him, unexpectedly. He had been in the grocery store, N.J.'s, the neighborhood one with wood floors where you could sign a charge sheet and they would send your parents a bill at the end of the month. A mother and her little girl were at the checkout in front of him. The little girl wanted to whisper something. Her mother leaned over and listened, then said to the cashier, "She's excited because she has a new toy cash register at home. She says, maybe when she grows up, she can run a real one."

The cashier laughed. She said, "I used to play with a toy cash register when I was little, too. And see? My dream came true."

She was entirely pleasant and cheerful saying this and yet, there was some other kind of knowledge in it, too. A knowledge that it sure as hell wasn't her dream come true, but, oh well, here she was.

There was some kind of "Totally Fine" clue there, but it was such a good line itself that Hector decided to save it for its own song. He wrote, "And see? My dream came true" in his notebook. That one could have a million verses.

He still didn't know what the verses would be for "Totally Fine," so he fiddled around with chords and notes, looking for a tune. Periodically he went into the refrain.

He was also thinking about his voice. Finding his own voice. Liz had talked about it the night of the coffeehouse, but Hector wasn't sure what it meant. Did you have to just take it as it came out of your throat? If you tried to improve it, or try out some other kind of voice, was that fake, or could it all be part of your own voice?

He tried singing "Totally Fine" in a slow, deep, gravelly voice. Then a falsetto. Papa Bear, Mama Bear. He felt silly. He sang it in a sarcastic, angry shout, which he knew wasn't his voice, but it was kind of fun so he did it several times, standing up and really slamming the chords. He jumped up and down a little and spun around.

Rowanne was standing in the doorway watching him.

"It's just you," she said. "It sounded like more."

It bothered Patty that electrons were so constantly in motion. It made the whole world seem like a place on the verge of disintegration. What if the molecules in this chair suddenly got all excited and spun apart? What if they realigned themselves and decided to be something other than wood? It was one of the many areas of science that she preferred not to think about: the very small (atoms) because they were so busy, and the very large (universe, infinity, time) because they were so unending.

Also relativity and the universe turning back in on itself, whatever that was supposed to mean. Picture a man on a train, picture trees going by. Yeah, sure. It was nothing like those things.

She was going to have to take her chances on actual people in trains with actual trees going by because the other stuff, the guy who gets younger because time is moving sideways next to his train, which science teachers seemed to feel was so exciting, made her feel like there was no ground beneath her feet. It gave her the creeps.

Patty wondered if her aversion to these ideas would relegate her to a job pouring coffee at a diner in The Future. She hoped the diner would be on earth. She hoped the coffee would be real. And the cups. And how soon was all of this going to really kick in? She glanced over her shoulder at her room to make sure that it hadn't reconfigured itself while her back was turned. She went downstairs and called Debbie on the phone, letting their conversation block out any thoughts about the expanding and compacting molecules that were simulating Debbie's voice in her ear.

The grass was still wet from the rain that had fallen earlier in the day, but the twilight sky was clearing and, in the west, an evening star hung a few inches above a deep pink and orange fringe, tail end of the sunset. Russell's sneakers were getting soaked. He lifted the lid, dropped the garbage in, and pressed the lid back on firmly to keep the raccoons from getting into it. He saw that a Styrofoam cup had fallen outside the can and, when he bent to pick it up, something else caught his eye.

It was some sort of a necklace, a slender chain with flat gold letters linked together in the middle of it. He thought it was probably something belonging to his little sister, Annette, but when he held it up in the fading light, the letters seemed to spell *Debbie*. He took it into the house, into the bright light of the kitchen. It still spelled *Debbie*. There was a tiny red gemstone dotting the *I*.

Russell wondered what the necklace was doing in his backyard, how it had gotten there, and which Debbie it belonged to. There were a lot of Debbies. Three that he knew of; probably there were even more. He pictured himself going around to all the Debbies, asking them if this was their necklace. "I found this in my backyard, is it yours?" He didn't want to do it. He decided he would turn it in to Lost and Found at school, and he put it in the pocket of his jacket, hanging in the hall closet. Where it stayed for a while, because the next day was sunny and warm.

But back in the evening before the sunny day, Phil was shooting baskets. He had finished his homework at school. Lenny heard the ball bouncing on cement and boinging on the backboard, and went over. He sat on the low wall in Phil's backyard while Phil kept shooting. Sometimes one or the other of them would say something, not saying much, but with the feeling of talking that is a good prelude for going home and going to bed.

A while later, when he finally did slip into his bed, Lenny felt a weight on his feet. Oops, he thought. He reached down and dropped his unopened school books onto the floor. As he fell asleep, he heard the muffled thunk of heavy objects settling into new positions down in the basement.

CHAPTER 17

At the Tastee-Freez on a Tuesday Evening

Three or four stars were visible in the opalescent dome of the sky, which was light and diaphanous to the west, a deepening delphinium blue to the east. The air was as warm as bathwater. Across the street, strings of lightbulbs illuminated rows of shiny used cars and a yellow sign with red letters that read

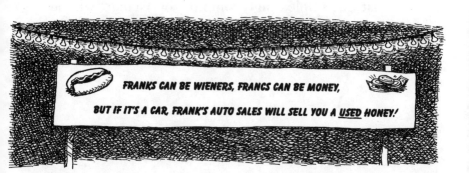

FRANKS CAN BE WIENERS, FRANCS CAN BE MONEY,

BUT IF IT'S A CAR, FRANK'S AUTO SALES WILL SELL YOU A <u>USED</u> HONEY!

Debbie couldn't look at the sign without saying it aloud in her head and trying to make it come out right. She and Patty were eating hot fudge sundaes from plastic boats with plastic spoons. They sat balanced on the back of a bench with their feet on the seat, watching people come and go at the Tastee-Freez. Light, spotty currents of east and westbound traffic shoop-shooped past, one way and the other.

Frank's Featured Cream Puff of the Week was a light blue Mustang convertible, a coupe. It reminded Patty of Nancy Drew, who she hadn't thought about for years.

"Did you ever notice," she said, "that everything good or interesting happens to Nancy Drew, and her friends just get the leftovers? If there's a statue or a painting or a lookalike person, it always looks like Nancy. It never looks like Bess or George."

"And they never mention Bess without saying that she's 'pleasingly plump,' or George without saying that she's boyish and athletic and has short hair," said Debbie. "Just so you don't forget that

Nancy is the beautiful one with the perfect figure and the 'titian' hair."

"What I want to know is, where does she find time to learn how to do so many things? You never see her practicing. If there's something she doesn't already know how to do, she's good at it right away. It's always harder for Bess and George."

"I'd like to read a book about Bess and George solving a crime while Nancy is in the hospital with a broken leg."

"Or off on a ski weekend with Ned."

"She's good at skiing."

"She's really, really good. She could probably be in the Olympics. Maybe she breaks her leg, though. An evil criminal rams her into a tree on the ski slope. And Bess and George solve the mystery without her."

"Ned could help."

"Maybe Hannah Gruen could still be in the story. She makes really good food."

"She could help, too. They could all help. And

they would find out that Nancy isn't the only one who can do things."

"Meanwhile, in her hospital bed, in traction, Nancy is studying marine biology. And Norwegian."

"And brain surgery."

"Have you ever noticed how many evil criminals use River Heights for their headquarters?"

"I know. It sounds like a scary place. I would be afraid to leave the house."

"Maybe you wouldn't be afraid if you had a light blue coupe."

A bobbing group of people rose into view. Their heads appeared first as they came up over the rise, then their shoulders and torsos, followed by their guitar cases, legs, and feet. There were eight or nine of them, traveling on foot, as a group. Debbie and Patty held their empty plastic boats and watched as the strolling guitarists set their cases down around a picnic table, then lined up at the two windows to order.

Hector was there. They were both about to call out to him and wave, but something stopped them. Their half-parted lips opened no farther, and their half-raised hands fell back to their laps.

He was talking to a girl, a girl neither of them had seen before. Talking to her from her other side was Dan Persik. Dan, the handsome. The girl was pretty in a way that made Debbie feel the hopelessness of both Hector's cause—because it was clear he was interested in her—and her own. Because it was clear that Dan was interested in her, too. She was petite and rounded and tan. She had an unruly mass of chestnut hair, pulled back in a loose bundle. She had large, dark eyes rimmed with long lashes. And dimples. She even had dimples.

She wore, along with cutoffs and a T-shirt, red platform sandals and an ankle bracelet. Debbie looked down at her own footwear: a pair of beat-up sneakers.

Also in Hector's subgroup was a second girl, who was a little older. Sixteen or seventeen. She accompanied them with the friendly, disinterested air of a baby-sitter.

Presently there came the sounds of guitar cases unsnapping and the bonking of guitars being removed, random bumpings of strings blooming from the acoustic wooden shells, followed by a brief jangly tuning, and Debbie's and Patty's attention was drawn to the other subgroup. Russell Kebbesward was in this group, sitting on a picnic table bench with two older people. Mr. Schimpf and a lady with white hair and half-moon glasses. Their leader was a young, frizzy-haired minister. You could tell he was a minister because he wore a short-sleeved black shirt with one of those collars. He stood with one foot up on a bench, his guitar hanging from his shoulder by means of a colorful embroidered strap.

The four of them began singing "Edelweiss," from the movie *The Sound of Music*. The minister sang the chord changes in between the words. His voice was froglike, yet sonorous.

"Have you ever noticed how much Seldem is like Austria?" murmured Patty.

A car rolled by on the street, the subwoofers of its sound system thumping like a giant heart.

"I think the guys in that car were Austrian," said Debbie.

"No, really," said Patty. "With the mountains and everything."

Hector's subgroup had been delayed in getting their cones by some other customers who wandered in front of them, but now three of his group sat at a picnic table near the singers, licking their cones. Hector alone remained at the window, pinning his wallet to the counter with the elbow of his cone-holding hand while with his other hand he tried to work the change back inside.

He had wanted to treat Meadow, but he hadn't been able to figure out how to do it without also treating Dan Persik and Meadow's cousin Robin. He didn't mind paying for Robin's cone, but he couldn't quite believe he had funded Dan Persik, who was now seated in a favorable position next to Meadow.

The whole thing was going wrong. Starting with when he invited Meadow to go for ice cream and Pastor Don overheard him. Pastor Don took it for a general invitation and broadcast it to the whole class. Everyone thought it was a great idea. Walking over, Dan Persik had proved himself expert at sidewalk maneuvering, and Hector conceded to himself that maybe football training might have practical applications after all. Now this. He wished Rowanne were here to tell him what to do.

Debbie and Patty sat for a few minutes more, each with a wadded-up paper napkin held loosely in her hand. Then they stood, tossing the crumpled napkins, the plastic boats, and spoons lightly into the trash basket as they passed. They caught Hector's eye and gave a little wave, and they heard the frizzy minister say they ought to do this every week.

Russell K. saw them toss their napkins, so lightly and easily, into the basket. They didn't even stop walking to do it. He thought that looked so graceful. He admired it the way you admire a waterfall or a sunset, or how someone plays a piece of music.

He closed his guitar case and reached for the jacket his mother had insisted he bring along, even though it was practically summer ("It's going to be chilly later."). He picked it up at the collar by two fingers and twirled it around, over one shoulder, in what he thought might be a similarly graceful move. But he hadn't properly gauged his distance from his classmates and the twirling jacket knocked Mary's glasses right off her face. She wasn't angry, or hurt, but she did cry out in surprise, and then there was the searching for one of the lenses, which had popped out, and no one, or almost no one, noticed the contents of the jacket pockets sailing through the air.

A wrapped stick of gum flew straight up and fell uneventfully down.

Some loose change arrived at a variety of locations, with a variety of semi-musical pings.

A cigarette lighter Russell had found somersaulted to the edge of the pavement, where it fell in with a crowd of other lost cigarette lighters and some black plastic combs.

And a necklace hurled itself toward the picnic bench where Hector was talking to Meadow, trying to make up for lost time. But it was Dan Persik who saw it land. He reached down and picked it up. He wondered why Russell was carrying around a necklace that said *Debbie*. Maybe that was his little sister's name. There were a lot of Debbies. There was, for instance, Debbie Pelbry, who had been at the Tastee-Freez a few minutes ago, whose locker was next to his. Who had, he was pretty sure, a crush on him. He could make her blush just by looking at her. It was kind of fun. Thinking maybe he could have some fun with this necklace, he put it in his pocket.

CHAPTER 18
In and Out of the Cocoon

When the idea came to Debbie that she needed a room of her own, and she was talking her parents into letting her have "the spare room," an alcove off the living room that barely qualified as its own room, because it was the only other room there was, they pointed out how small it was. They pointed out that there was no door between the little room and the living room, just an arched opening in the wall. And they pointed out that the piano had to stay in there, because there was nowhere else for it to go.

Debbie, focused on her vision, said that was all okay; she didn't mind. So her mother made a drape and hung it from a rod inside the room, and they moved Debbie's bed and desk downstairs from the room she had always shared with Chrisanne.

She didn't admit to anyone that once all the furniture was in there, the room felt smaller than she had thought it would. It was only slightly more spacious than a storage locker, which it resembled, furniture arrangement-wise. Everything was right up against everything else. There was a small empty space in the center of the room where Debbie could stand up or sit down. Sitting down had to be done with crossed legs, or at least with bent knees.

Still, sitting cross-legged in the middle of the floor, or on her bed, she felt she had found something. A sanctuary, though she didn't know from what. A secret entryway. To go where? She didn't know that, either.

The room had a small closet, which she had to

share with a few of everyone's out-of-season clothes, some winter boots, and a couple of boxes.

One of the boxes, a round hatbox, held Helen

Pelbry's collection of small figurines from when she was Helen Brandt. They were wrapped in tissue paper that had been wrapped and unwrapped so many times that it was soft and crepey with folds and wrinkles. The figurines were all dogs, of different breeds and made of different materials. Some porcelain, some wooden, some glass.

There was a small, heavy, rounded one with perky rounded ears, made of solid iron with blue-gray paint that had begun to chip and fall off, revealing dark metal and the beginnings of rust. There was another sitting dog, also of a geometric breed, but this one was tall and triangular, of creamy porcelain with polka-spots in undoglike colors: persimmon and yellow and lime green. A dog that had been carved barking straight up into the air to fit into the rectangular shape of a block of wood. A carved Irish setter, painted china collies, black and white Scottie dogs that were salt and pepper shakers. There was a whimsical dachshund, twisted and snipped from a hot glass rod, light and delicate. A marble schnauzer. A brass poodle.

Her mother never got them out and looked at them, as far as she knew. Debbie was the one who had unwrapped and wrapped them all those times, since first discovering the box when she was six or seven. She liked taking them out and looking at them. When she asked about them, her mother said they were just souvenirs; there was nothing special about them. All the same, she didn't want Debbie to keep them out. She didn't exactly say why.

Debbie arranged them on her desk, then wrapped them up again and put the box back down in the closet. Then she hauled out the other box and lifted it onto her bed.

This was also her mother's. It was a cardboard carton filled with scrapbooks, yearbooks, photo albums, and other odds and ends from Helen Pelbry's youth, her life before marriage.

In the official photo albums, the ones that were kept in the bookcase in the living room, Helen had a brief childhood. She began as a toddler in white muslin, trimmed with lace. Standing in a doorway, her chubby hand on the doorknob, her serious face and her little hand in a wash of sunlight. She was momentarily a ten-year-old, in braids and a cowgirl outfit. A senior in high school, pretty and composed in a sweater and a string of pearls. And then suddenly a bride, in a white satin dress with tiny satin-covered buttons from her wrist to her elbow, and down her spine. All of this happened in black and white, on three pages.

The cardboard box had more information, though still not enough. Debbie wasn't sure what she was looking for, what she needed to know. Helen Brandt's seventeen-year-old face smiled out of the yearbook page. She looked lively and confident. She looked poised. In some ways the past looked like a nicer place than the present. More golden, even in black and white, with less cruddiness. Probably that wasn't true. She had heard about the Depression, polio and scarlet fever. About her grandfather coming home from work with his white collar gone gray, from all the soot and ash, just in the air, from the steel mills.

Still, the girl in the picture looked like she knew

how to make things be golden for her. How did she do it? Maybe that's what Debbie wanted to know.

She pulled a wad of pamphlets and programs out of the box, propped her pillow against the headboard, and leaned back. The one on top was a booklet of instructions for crocheting lacy collars  to set on top of a sweater or a dress. It seemed a little like putting glitter on a grocery bag, but many people in those days only had one sweater or one dress. It was hard to believe, but that's what her mother said, and that's how they spruced up for special occasions.

The next booklet in the pile was a collection of recipes for faded holiday cookies, followed by a book put out by an aluminum foil company that showed a myriad of creative ways in which foil could be used, mostly unrelated to cooking and requiring dozens of square yards of foil. The effects were pretty spectacular. A swan centerpiece, for example, molded from crushed foil, holding a red rose in its beak, placed on a green tablecloth that was reflected, along with the light from two white candles, in every crinkle of the foil.

As she flipped through a calendar year of special occasions expressed in aluminum, the voices of her mother and their neighbor Fran entered the living room from the direction of the kitchen and filtered in through the flowered curtain.

"I wouldn't worry about it, Helen," said Fran. "It might never happen."

"I'm not worried, really," said Helen. "It kind of makes you wonder, though."

The sound of squeaking couch springs. They were settling in for a chat.

Debbie picked up a program from the premiere screening of the movie *Gone with the Wind*. Apparently it had been a big deal. The program was fifty pages thick.

"By the way," Helen was saying. "Did I tell you

that Debbie is going to go down to old Mrs. Bruning's house on Saturdays, to help her out with housework? I guess she's getting very arthritic."

Debbie's ears pricked up when she heard her name and she half-listened to her mother's version of the story. She usually sounded pretty good in her mother's stories, though not quite like herself. The stories themselves were that way, too; more entertaining than what really happened, though close enough that you could think, oh, so that's how it was, even if you had been there and it hadn't seemed that way at all. You could find out in this way that something you thought had been a disaster had actually come out quite well.

In her mother's version of the Mrs. Bruning story, Debbie was a take-charge kind of girl who saw a frail old woman in distress and went right to the rescue.

She didn't mind being cast by her mother as a heroine. But the way it happened was more accidental. And it was more equal.

👀

Mrs. Bruning lived in one of the older houses near
the bottom of Prospect Hill Road.
Her house was on a corner lot,
facing the side street. As you
walked past it, up or down the hill,
you could see into the backyard.
The yard slanted up steeply away
from a concrete patio, which was
shaded by a corrugated fiberglass awning of faded
yellow, held up by metal bars that enclosed
ornamental scrolls, painted black, barnacled with
scabs of rust. The house was built of gray stone and
had a castle-y appearance, if you could sift it out
from the awning, and the big doorway that had been
fitted with plywood to accommodate a small modern
door with a crescent-shaped window, the bent and
cockeyed venetian blinds hanging behind the
leaded and stained glass windows, and the sun porch
tacked onto one side, shingled up to the windows
with roofing shingles in variegated shades of purple,
brown, and green.

Despite all of its prostheses, Debbie thought that the ivy climbing up the stone, and the stained glass, and the small porchlike recess on the second floor with the crenellated half-wall gave the house an elegance and a personality. She had always wondered what it was like inside.

She saw Mrs. Bruning out in her backyard and waved. Mrs. Bruning waved back. Then she held her hand up, as if to say "Wait a minute," and started making her way purposefully across the grass. She was short and solid, bottle-shaped. A bottle of vinegar, or  Pepto-Bismol, with legs. She was one of those elderly women whose cleavage starts about two inches below her collarbone and your main response to it is an intellectual curiosity about how that can even physically work.

She moved toward Debbie with determination, but her steps were small, baby steps, and effortful, as if each one was costing her. It was a big yard, so

Debbie stepped into it and walked over to meet her, to save time. Not that she was saving it for anything in particular.

Debbie knew two things about Mrs. Bruning. One was that she had never cut her hair. At least that's what people said. It may or may not have been true, but her hair seemed as if it might be pretty long. She wore it in a heavy braid arranged around her head in a complicated way, held in place with bobby pins. The hair closest to her scalp was white and fluffy, but as the braid narrowed, it became carrot colored, then dwindled into a faded russet wisp weaving in and out of the pin-prickled coronet. It wouldn't have been that surprising to see baby birds peeping out over the top of it.

The other thing Debbie knew was that, when Mrs. Bruning's husband was still alive, the two of them had owned and operated the Idle Hour Restaurant. They were German. From Germany German. Although they had been in America for a long time.

"It's going to rain," said Mrs. Bruning as they met. She was short. She only came up to Debbie's shoulder. It was an odd sensation, looking down at someone you felt you ought to be looking up to. Debbie was fairly certain Mrs. Bruning had been larger, in the past.

She looked at the sky, a dropped ceiling of soft gray wool. The air had a pre-rain stillness to it.

"Yeah," she said. She said it pleasantly, but immediately wished she had said, "Yes," or even "Yes, ma'am." Mrs. Bruning had that effect.

"Yes," she corrected herself. "I think it is. Going to rain."

"I can't get my laundry down from the clothesline," said Mrs. Bruning.

"Oh?" said Debbie. She still thought they were just making conversation.

"Why not?" she asked. It seemed like the logical next line in the conversation.

"My hands," said Mrs. Bruning. "And my shoulders. Arthritis. For some reason they were working better this morning, I was able to hang it all up. But now they are so stiffened up on me, I can't do it. I can't get the laundry down. And it's going to rain."

She looked at Debbie expectantly. She demonstrated how her arms would only go so high, how her hands would not do what she needed them to do.

"You see what I'm saying?" she said. She had bright brown eyes, like a bird's eyes.

She didn't actually ask for help, but Debbie finally realized what she was supposed to do here. She glanced at the lowered sky, the waiting laundry, and Mrs. Bruning's knotted hands.

"Oh," she said. "Let me help you."

The first cold heavy drops of rain fell on Debbie's shoulders as she carried Mrs. Bruning's laundry into the house, where it was dark. Gray light hovered outside the windows, but it couldn't penetrate the ivy. Debbie bent awkwardly over her burden, the big basket, piled high.

"Where should I put this?" she asked. "I mean, where would you like it?"

"Just in here," said Mrs. Bruning. She made her bulky way past the hall-filling obstacle of Debbie and the laundry and, a few seconds later, a switch clicked and a light came on over a kitchen sink.

"The overhead bulb is burnt out," she explained. "I can't reach it without climbing up on a chair, and then I'm afraid of falling. Just put it in the corner, on the floor. I will take care of it later."

Debbie nudged aside a small stack of newspapers with her foot and set the basket down. She stood up and turned around. The dimly lit kitchen seemed at first to be a cluttered, disorganized mess. But as her eyes adjusted, she saw spotlessly clean surfaces. Polished fixtures. The impression of disorder came from a variety of projects that Mrs. Bruning had not managed to complete. A bag of groceries sitting on one of the chairs was only half unloaded, and what had been removed from it had only made it as far as the tabletop. Next to the cans of soup, standing in tidy rows along with a box of cereal and a loaf of bread, an old typewriter held a letter in progress. Just beyond that, a neatly folded pile of bathroom towels, pink with roses, waited to be delivered to a closet somewhere in the murky house. A glass of milk and a plate with a partially eaten jelly sandwich sat nearby with a folded paper napkin tucked under its edge like a still life. On the counter by the wall were two boxes that had been neatly labeled "Christmas Ornaments: Attic." The room was full of efforts abandoned in midstream.

Mrs. Bruning caught Debbie's gaze and laughed. She picked up the glass and the dish with the jelly sandwich and carried them to the sink.

"And then again," she said. "Maybe I won't." Over her shoulder, she added, "I'm going to have to think about it."

Rain pelted the windows; the kitchen felt cozy. Yellow light from the shaded lamp illuminated a calendar printed on a dishtowel hanging on the wall.

The months, and the verse above them, were in German. Debbie was in her second year of German, and she could tell that the rhyme was about baking a cake, though she didn't know all of the words.

"*'Schieb, schieb in Ofen nein,'*" she read aloud. "Why does it say not to put it in the oven?"

Mrs. Bruning looked at the dishtowel, then back at Debbie.

"It's not *nein* as in 'no,'" she said. "It's a shortened way of saying *hinein*, which means 'in there.' As in, 'shove it in there.' A colloquialism. A slang word."

"I didn't think German would have slang words," said Debbie. "It always sounds so precise. Except for the *schl* and *ch* sounds."

Mrs. Bruning chuckled. "I can guarantee you," she said, "we are as lazy as anyone else. Just take a look around you."

Debbie did.

"I can change your lightbulb for you," she said.

And while she did that, Mrs. Bruning put the

kettle on the stove to make tea, and fished a package of vanilla sandwich cremes out of the grocery bag on the chair. That's how it had started: they liked each other.

Debbie tossed the *Gone with the Wind* program on the "done" pile and picked up a pamphlet called "Just Us Girls." She had looked at it before; she had looked at all of them before. This one had a drawing of three females on the cover, a mother and two daughters sitting close together on a sofa. All three were drinking from the type of mug that might hold hot cocoa. Wavy lines indicating steam and warmth rose out of the cups. The mother and the younger daughter, who wore braids, were both in their nightgowns, robes, and slippers, and were listening intently to the teenaged daughter, who sat between them in a beautiful evening gown. The idea was that she had just returned from a big date. She looked like the kind of girl who would have big dates frequently.

The pamphlet had been put out by a sanitary napkin company, so there was a lot of information about periods, and which company's products were best to use. Some of this information was not very modern, since the pamphlet was thirty or forty years old. It talked a lot about being modern, though, and how lucky a thing it was to be modern. It seemed to suggest that emergence from the Dark Ages had been recent, a narrow escape facilitated largely by the sanitary napkin industry.

There were also sections on health, grooming, and how to be popular. The popularity section was big on "confidence." Debbie didn't feel a need to be popular, but she thought she would like to feel confident. The information on how to do this was vague. It mentioned being friendly, having good manners, and being clean and neat. She already did all that. Maybe not the neat part.

But perhaps the exercises in the health section would help.

She positioned the pamphlet, open to the

exercise page, on her bed and moved to the epicenter of her room. By extending her legs past the desk into the space between her bed and the closet, she was able to do sit-ups. And leg raises. A breeze. She stood up and aligned herself for toe touches. All of the exercises were easy. Confidence was oozing through her. The challenge was in doing the exercises without banging into the furniture. She stood in the small hollow of her cocoon and did arm circles. Small ones, and medium. Large were not possible.

She wondered if the confident feeling only lasted while you were actually doing the exercises. That could be inconvenient, and awkward.

Yesterday, for example. The last day of school, everyone clearing out their lockers of hairbrushes, gym clothes, mirrors, photos, and magazine pictures. They had to peel off all the tape. The lockers were going to be inspected.

Debbie had a lot of tape to peel off, and she concentrated on that so as not to be undone by the protracted nearness of Dan Persik. She had, of course, tried to think of something to say, something really funny or interesting that would get his attention and reveal her true self. She was mistaken in thinking that's what it would take, but she was thinking it.

She pictured herself, now, pausing in her tape peeling to do a few arm circles. It would be hard to explain. Maybe she could have repaired to the restroom for a few minutes, to do them there.

But she hadn't. She had just peeled away silently, adding pathetic scraggly layers to her sticky little ball of tape.

A funny thing had happened, though. Involving Dan Persik. When they were almost done, he had said, "Oh, hey—Debbie." She had looked up (startled bunny look) from where she was kneeling. He smiled and said, "I have something for you."

He fished in every pocket of his jeans, then went through them all again, even pulling his front pockets inside out. Debbie waited, unable to imagine what would happen next. Something good? Something embarrassing? Her heart hopped up and down.

"Jeez," he said. "What did I do with it?"

He went around once more, then said, "I guess I lost it. Never mind. It was just something I found. I thought you might like it."

There was a teasing note to his voice. Debbie didn't know what to think.

She smiled, shrugged, and said, "Oh, well." She thought she was quite cool, under the circumstances.

Mr. Dysleski arrived at her locker, glanced at it, and told her she could go.

"Have a nice summer," he said.

"Yeah, have a nice summer, Debbie," said Dan. "See you around."

"Thanks," she said. "You, too."

And walked down the hall and out through the doors into summer vacation. A place and time that promised many pleasures. But it didn't look like romance was going to be one of them.

She put the pamphlet back into the box, the box back into the closet, stretched out on her bed, and gazed up at the blank movie screen of the ceiling. The white walls of her cocoon. The blank, arid desert of the summer.

The voices of her mother and Fran, which had blurred into a murmur, now disentangled themselves and spoke alternately and distinctly.

"I wonder if Mike will win again today," said Fran.

"I hope he doesn't," said Helen. "He's won enough. It's someone else's turn."

They were heading down to the basement. It was time for *Jeopardy*.

Debbie went out onto the front porch. Maybe a change of scenery would help. Maybe a miracle would help. Maybe nothing would help.

CHAPTER NINETEEN

Where the Necklace Went

The necklace had escaped from Dan's pocket by working its way through a hole, a young hole, not yet big enough for a coin to pass through. He felt a light tickling sensation on his thigh as the chain bounced against it, waiting for the letters to be jolted out, but he didn't pay attention to it; his thoughts were elsewhere.

As he walked down the street on the morning of the last day of school, he passed Hector's house and smiled to himself, thinking about last night at the Tastee-Freez.

Sorry, Hector, he thought cheerfully. Old buddy, old pal.

The back end of Rowanne's old beater was poking out over the sidewalk, and as Dan made an exaggerated movement to juke around it, the necklace slipped down his pants leg and fell out onto the ground.

A minute or two later a couple of little girls spotted it. After some discussion, they decided that whoever had lost it would find it more easily if they put it on the trunk lid of the car, closer to eye level.

For twenty minutes it remained there.

Then Rowanne, running late, burst through the front door and down the steps, leaped into the driver's seat, and sped away. The necklace shimmied back and forth over the lid of the trunk as the car stopped at stop signs, then surged forward again. Somewhere in the middle of Prospect Hill Road, it dove from the car onto a freshly poured ribbon of road-patch tar. The gold letters of Debbie's name hit the tar, sank in at a variety of angles, and waited to be run over.

CHAPTER 20

Hair

I

Hector was letting his hair grow. Rowanne had mentioned in passing that he looked like a buffalo. He didn't think she necessarily meant this in a bad way.

II

The third time Debbie went to Mrs. Bruning's house, Mrs. Bruning asked Debbie to cut off her hair.

"It's too hard for me even to wash it," she said. "Cut it all off, except leave me an inch and a half or maybe two inches all over."

Just pulling out the bobby pins and unwinding the two braids from around the old woman's head took a while. Unwound, they fell down over her bosom and her lap, to a little past her knees. She looked like a very old milkmaid.

"Go ahead and chop them off," she said. "I can't wait."

"Do you want me to put a rubber band at the top of the braids, so you can save them?" asked Debbie.

Mrs. Bruning said, with a snort, "What would I save them for?"

Debbie didn't know what you would save them for, but she thought that tossing them in the trash was going to feel sacrilegious. Though keeping them would feel creepy. Putting them out so that birds could use the hair in their nests would probably result in frustrated birds grounded by hair-entangled feet. So she chopped them off and dropped them in the plastic wastebasket under the sink, on top of the used tissues and coffee grounds. She half expected them to rebel, to rise up like cobras or cast indignant spells from where they lay. But as far as she could tell, they stayed put.

The next step was to trim the remaining hair all over. Mrs. Bruning didn't want a style, or anything she would have to fuss with. She was done with fussing. She wanted it all short and out of the way.

As she snipped, Debbie grew alarmed at the sparseness of what was left. Pink scalp was plainly visible under the white fluff. In some places, particularly right in front where it was most noticeable, there was almost more pink than white. Even though she had only followed Mrs. Bruning's instructions, she felt queasy. She felt like a vandal. She had a panicky desire to laugh, not out of mirth but hysteria. She swallowed it. She had single-handedly sheared away Mrs. B.'s dignity and left her half bald.

"It's pretty thin," she said nervously. She had the

thought that maybe they could still retrieve the braids, shake off the coffee grounds, and wrap them around Mrs. B's head.

"You're worried," observed Mrs. Bruning. "Let me see. Go and get my mirror, from on my dresser."

Debbie went, and returned with the mirror. Mrs. Bruning took it and looked in, moving it up and down and from side to side. Her face was unreadable.

"It's the new me," she said finally. Then she quoted the Reverend Doctor Martin Luther King, Jr., who she admired. "'Free at last, free at last,'" she said in her German accent instead of his southern one. "'Great God A'mighty, I'm free at last.'"

CHAPTER 21

Confession

"Hey, Lenny," said Phil, "did you go to confession today?"

He was going to ask next whether Lenny had seen that the wooden boxes were on, over all the statues of the saints. It was because the carnival was coming up. Phil had always thought the boxes were to protect the statues from accidental damage while the courtyard was thronged with people, but this morning someone at the church told him that they were to keep the saints from seeing people playing games of chance. Because it was the same as gambling. He didn't know if it was true, but he thought it was a funny idea. Like putting a bag over God's head.

That's why he brought it up, that's what he was going to say, but he never said it, because Lenny said no, he was working over at the garage all morning, and then Patty said, "So, what do you guys confess when you go to confession?

"I mean," she went on, "do you have to say every little thing, or just really bad things, like murder? Or coveting your neighbor's wife or something?"

She was asking Lenny and Phil. They were the Catholics. Phil just looked at her, but Lenny was willing to give it a shot.

"Well," he said, "do you know about venial and mortal sins?"

"No," said Patty. "I've heard of mortal sins, but not venial ones. I don't think we have those at our church. We just say at the same time how basically sinful and unclean we all are. Which I don't really believe. So if you think about it, I'm telling a lie when I'm supposed to be trying to be holy."

Phil's thoughts had skipped from the upcoming carnival to other upcoming events.

"Seldem Days is next week, too," he said. "Next Saturday."

He was about to say how it was funny that it was called Seldem Day*s*, when it was only one day, but he didn't get to say it because Debbie said, "I have to go work for Mrs. Bruning."

And then Patty said, "Can't you switch it for another day?"

Debbie shrugged. "It's all right," she said. "I'll miss the parade, but I don't really care. It's pretty much the same every year. I can still go for the chicken dinner and the fireworks."

"I'll go," said Lenny.

"I'll go," said Patty.

"Me, too," said Hector. He was hoping to see Meadow there. He had told her about it at guitar class, at Rowanne's suggestion. He had been careful to mention it out of earshot of Pastor Don, so it wouldn't become another group event.

"Oh, yeah," said Meadow. "I already know about that. We'll probably come. Maybe I'll see you there."

She smiled at Hector, and her smile was like a warm summer day. Her eyes were like dancing stars. She looked like a peach with a suntan. He thought about her as he followed the others to the pickup.

Lenny climbed into his position in the driver's seat and turned the key. He jiggled it a little bit, took it out, put it back in, turned it again.

"Turn it on," said Phil.

"I can't," said Lenny.

"Why not?"

"I think the battery's dead."

He reached for a knob on the dashboard and turned it, with another click. "Someone left the lights on," he said. "I'm trying to remember if it was me. I hope not."

"We could listen on the patio," said Debbie. "On the transistor. It wouldn't be as good, but it would be all right."

"My dad is gonna be ticked," said Lenny. "He goes in to work at midnight tonight."

"Maybe you better tell him."

"He's asleep. I'd have to wake him up."

He hesitated, then he said, "Okay. We're gonna try something. I've helped my dad do it a couple of times. If it doesn't work, I'll go in and wake him up."

"What are we going to do?"

"We're going to push the truck till it starts rolling down the driveway, and Debbie's going to pop the clutch."

"I am?" said Debbie.

"How come Debbie gets to drive?" asked Phil.

"Because she's a girl. In case you hadn't noticed. She's too helpless and puny and weak to push. And besides, she knows how to work the clutch."

"How do you know that?" Hector asked Debbie.

"I showed her," said Lenny.

"How come you never showed me?" asked Phil.

"I don't know," said Lenny. "You never asked me, for cripes sake."

Debbie was thinking that she was not helpless or weak, but that she wanted to drive again, so she wasn't going to say anything about it.

"What should I do?" asked Patty. "I'm even punier than Debbie."

She was hoping not to have to help push.

"Go stand down by the street and make sure no one's coming," said Lenny.

"Okay," she said, and trotted off.

Lenny explained to Debbie what it was that she was supposed to do. He made it sound as uncomplicated as plugging a cord into an outlet. Maybe a little more complicated than that. But not a lot.

"What if it doesn't start?" she asked.

"Just put on the brake," said Lenny.

"Okay," she said. That was easy. She already knew how. "I'm ready. Go push."

👀

The three boys pushed several times before the truck budged even a little. The truck seemed determined to stay where it was. Lenny kept telling Phil and Hector where to stand, and where and when to push.

"I think I might be puny and weak and helpless, too," Hector announced hopefully.

He had new respect for the truck. He was willing to let the truck win.

Lenny grinned. "Shut up and push," he said.

They got it into a small rocking movement, and from inside the cab Debbie could hear Lenny saying, "This is good. Just keep doing it."

Her right hand was on the knob of the stick and her feet were in position. In her mind she went through what Lenny had told her to do. The truck began moving, in just one direction, not rocking anymore, but rolling down the gentle grade of the gravel driveway. Slowly, then a little faster. Methodically she followed Lenny's instructions. The truck was almost to the street when the engine turned over. She shifted into neutral, revved the engine a little, and put on the brakes just as the truck reached the other side of the street. A piece of cake. There was nothing to it. She saw Patty standing there and realized that she had forgotten to look to her to make sure no one was coming. Oops.

"It worked," she said to Lenny, as he arrived at the window.

"We got lucky," said Lenny.

"What do you mean, 'lucky'?" she asked.

"Nothing," he said. "It doesn't always work, that's all."

Lenny decided they should listen to the show while driving around the Boney Dump at the end of the street, to charge up the battery. When they got there, he decided he might as well teach Debbie how to do a three-point turn. They drove around and around, back and forth. Phil and Hector rode in the back, listening through the window that opened in the back of the cab.

Suddenly the sound of the engine sputtered and

died. The truck rolled to a quiet stop. Hector and Phil heard Lenny say, "Shit!" and then they heard him say, "Excuse me."

Phil called out, "What happened?"

"We're out of gas," said Lenny. "I can't believe it."

He got out and grabbed a gas can from the back, and they all set off across the cindery expanse, toward the next outpost of civilization, a low clump of trees and buildings where there was a Sinclair station.

As they crunched along over the cinders, Lenny fished in his pockets for money. He turned to Patty, who was crunching nearby, and said, "Do they have penance at your church?"

CHAPTER 22

Wuthering Heights/
Popular Mechanics

Debbie was reading *Wuthering Heights*. Physically, she was in the backyard under a tree, with more backyards in all directions but one, all cluttered with picnic tables, clotheslines, grills, garbage cans, lawn chairs,

Lenny was eating a ham sandwich at the kitchen table. He was reading about solenoids in *Popular Mechanics*, or trying to. Blinding stripes of sunlight blasting through the venetian wading pools, patios. Petunias. Tomato plants. Sprinklers. But otherwise, she was out on the moors with Catherine, crying Heathcliff's name out into the blinding storm. Their rough and wild childhood friendship had deepened into love, but Catherine had become engaged to someone else who was more educated, refined, and wealthy. And Heathcliff had gone away. There was more to it than that, but still, Debbie wondered at how Cathy could marry Linton. She didn't think money and refinement mattered to blinds were causing blinking afterimages to dance around in his eyeballs. It was a trippy effect. He reached for the string to adjust the angle of the slats. When they were horizontal, and his eyes stopped freaking out, he noticed that Debbie was sitting under the tree in the Pelbrys' backyard, reading a book. Lenny felt a neighborly urge to go do something in his own backyard. Work on the dirt bike, maybe. He set his her the way it did to Cathy. If she liked someone, she would like them. That was all that would matter.

She looked up from her book. Lenny was working on his dirt bike. She watched him for a few minutes. He was wearing a T-shirt with the sleeves chopped off, and she noticed that he had muscles in his arms. When had that happened, she wondered. Lenny had never been athletic. It must be related to the gearhead phase he was going through.

She wished for a dish in the sink, took what was left of the sandwich outside, and bounced down onto the patio where he sat on the old glider, chewing and looking at his bike. He wasn't sure what to do to it. It was already perfect. Just for fun, he decided he would change the front fork fluid.

Immediately he was absorbed in the pleasure of his task, only somewhat aware of the bright sun that poured down on his shoulders and made moment that she lived in another century, in another country, with moors and mansions and elegant ways of speaking and complicated romantic clothing: cloaks with hoods, velvet, riding boots. Wool shawls and handkerchiefs. A world where she didn't even know what all the words meant. Like, what was *dimity*? And what exactly was a fortnight? She hadn't gotten around to looking them up; she just guessed and kept reading.

A lot would depend, of course, on whether you him squint, and the concrete paving bricks under his knees that made him periodically shift his position. He decided he would also adjust the chain. He loosened the rear axle nut and the chain adjuster, moved the swing arm back to tighten the chain, then tightened the axle nut back up again. Finishing, Lenny realized he was thirsty and stood up. The backyard rematerialized. The lawn chair under the Pelbrys' tree were born in the mansion or the hovel.

And, if she had been born in another century, she would now be dead, and she liked it that she was, at this moment, alive.

Cathy, she thought, had never experienced the freedom of wearing cut-offs all summer. Of riding a bike. The pleasure of a Coke poured over ice. She went into the house to get one.

was empty. Something about that was disappointing. He looked at it for a minute without remembering why, then opened the screen door and went inside to get something to drink.

CHAPTER 23

The Childhood Friend

Debbie's thoughts drifted from the conversation. When they drifted back, it wasn't to listen, but to watch Phil's hands. She had never noticed how much he moved them around, talked with them, when he was excited about something, maybe because that was almost never. Normally he was so calm and even. Now his face was animated, and his hands darted and swooped like birds flying from perch to perch in the trees. She also noticed a mosquito bite starting to bleed down his forehead, like a war wound. But it was his hands that briefly hypnotized her. They were expressive, and she hadn't ever thought of Phil as expressive.

She felt she was seeing a hidden part of him. The thought came to her that maybe Phil was the childhood friend she was destined to fall in love with. As soon as she thought it, she saw him differently. She saw the handsomeness in his features, the interestingness of his personality. When Phil's eyes met hers, she looked away quickly, suddenly self-conscious. It was completely stupid, but there didn't seem to be anything she could do about it.

She looked at her knee, where there was a scabbed scratch. She looked at a rose-of-Sharon bush in Lenny's yard, lit to muted green brilliance on one side by the streetlight, the other side lost in the darkness. From up and down the street came ripples of conversations on porches.

Lenny was talking now and, listening once more, Debbie remembered the reason she had stopped paying attention in the first place. They were talking about a movie she hadn't seen, going into rapturous detail about car chases and explosions and secret agent–type stunts involving helicopters, boats, and doing things while dangling from ropes. Expressive hand gestures.

Debbie decided that Phil probably did have hidden depths, but this wasn't them. The romance, which had blossomed entirely inside her own head, faded. No one knew about it but her, and it all happened in less than five minutes. She was relieved that it was over, but now there was nothing to do but listen to the boring conversation.

Hector was sitting next to her on the curb. Patty had gone home a while ago. Hector appeared to be listening attentively to Lenny and Phil.

"Which do you like better," he said to Debbie. "Listening to people talk about movies you haven't seen, or listening to people try to remember what they dreamed last night?"

Debbie laughed.

"It always seems interesting when you're the one who's telling it, though," she said.

"That's true," said Hector. "My grandmother thinks people are really interested in hearing about all of her surgeries."

"My great-aunt thinks we really want to know that our fourth cousin got a job selling shoes in a department store."

"My mother thinks people really want to know how she made the Jell-O salad."

Debbie laughed again. "Probably some people do want to know that," she said. "My mother would want to know."

"Would you, though?" asked Hector.

"No," said Debbie. "But I would eat some if it's the kind that has those little mandarin oranges in it."

"It's not," said Hector. "It has grated carrots in it. And celery."

"Oh. Then I wouldn't eat some, I don't think."

A few honking guffaws came from Lenny and

Phil. They were still talking about their movie. Or something.

"So," said Hector, "have you had any interesting dreams lately?"

Debbie looked at him.

"I don't think I would tell you even if I did," she said.

CHAPTER 24

Grosi

Peter Bruning woke up and he didn't know where he was. He was in a strange bed, in a strange room. A strange-looking branch snaked by outside the window, maybe attached to whatever tree was filling the room with dim green humid light, or maybe not.

Somewhere not too far away, a vacuum cleaner whined and droned. The sound of it rose and sank as it turned corners, dove down under furniture and pulled back out, clattered from carpet onto the wood floor. Then it stopped. The room was now familiar, and Peter remembered that he was in his grandmother's house. Grosi's house. For *Grossmutter*. There was his suitcase on the floor, unlatched, airline tags sprouting from the handle.

He remembered now that he and his parents had stopped here last night on their way from the airport to his aunt and uncle's house, where they stayed during their visits. They never stayed at Grosi's. There were various reasons for this, but the main one was that she drove Peter's father, who was her son, nuts. It was a mutual feeling. He drove her nuts, too. Peter's mother's theory was that they were too much alike. They were both alpha males. That was her joke.

Grosi had made dinner for them, roast beef and potatoes with gravy. Carrots and cabbage. Corn pudding with heavy cream. Lettuce with hot bacon and bacon grease on it. Tapioca with canned peaches in syrup.

After dinner, as Peter's parents tried to cancel

out the heaviness of the meal by taking their coffee black, they brought up the topic they had been talking about with each other, and over the phone with the aunts and uncles, in the preceding weeks. The topic of how Grosi might want to move into an apartment. Where everything was all on one floor. She wouldn't have to climb steps and it wouldn't be so much work to take care of. It would be so much easier for her, with her arthritis and everything else.

There was that Senior Citizens Tower they were putting up in Birdvale, what about that? It looked really nice, and it was so close to everything. The grocery store, the post office. A bank. She wouldn't even have to drive.

As they talked, Peter watched his grandmother, and he could see that his grandmother would rather drop dead. She sat like a stone, her hands folded in her lap. A ruse to conceal the fact that she could no longer completely unfold them.

"I'm fine here," she said. "I have someone

coming to help me with things. A girl. She comes once a week."

"A girl can't do everything that needs to be done around here, Mother," said Peter's father. "What about your windows? If you don't get paint on them, they're going to rot. There are three years of leaves in your gutters; they're about to fall off the house. And you need a new roof. A girl coming once a week can't do all of that."

"I could," said Peter. "I mean, I bet I could do some of it. A lot of it. Maybe not the roof."

He hadn't planned to say it. It just came out.

His mother ignored him.

"And what if you fall," she said. "What about your sugar, and your heart?"

Grosi ignored her. She turned to Peter.

"Why don't you stay here with me for a few days?" she said. "Can you do that? You can do a few little jobs for me, then tell everyone how fine I am."

She was asking him for help. She needed an ally. She needed her house. If you put her in an anonymous little apartment somewhere, she might disappear. Evaporate. Peter couldn't believe his parents were even suggesting it.

"Okay, Grosi," he said. "I can stay here all week."

He felt he was honoring an ancient, unspoken pact.

His father raised his eyebrows. His mother just looked at him. When they left for the evening, Peter followed them out to get his bag from the car.

"It's just postponing the inevitable," he heard his father say.

"Let him spend a week here," said his mother. "Then he'll see."

That's why he was here. He reached for his glasses and looked around the room for a clock. He didn't feel quite as noble as he had last night. He would be here for one week, and he didn't really know what he would be able to do. He hadn't had much experience at being useful.

❧

Mrs. Bruning had trouble falling asleep. She couldn't stop thinking about the conversation with her son and the California wife. Three times she turned on the bedside lamp and read, trying to put it out of her thoughts so she could drift off. Twice she tried the *Reader's Digest*. Usually she found it very useful as a sleeping aid. The first time she went through and read all of the funny stories. The second time she read quite a bit of the condensed novel at the end. It was a humorous one, which she liked better than the heartwarming or inspirational ones.

Both times she thought she had banished the conversation to the depths where it belonged, but each time it crept back in, hiding inside some innocent thought and then jumping out at her, like Trojan soldiers from their wooden horse.

She worked her way up once more to a sitting position and turned on the light. She put on her thick glasses and sat there, for a moment, looking around the room. She liked it, even in the semidarkness. Especially in the semidarkness. Dim lighting was better for old things. For old furniture and old people. For people as old as me, she thought, pitch black is probably best. She had a silent laugh at her little joke.

She didn't like new buildings. They didn't feel right to her. They didn't smell right or sound right. And she didn't want to have to go on an elevator every time she went in or out. Why should she be stranded in some claustrophobic white box up on the umpteenth floor, surrounded by senile nincompoops? She wasn't going to do it.

This Peter, this grandson she had barely recognized when he walked in the door, wanted to help her. She didn't know what he was capable of, but he was on her side. And the Debbie girl was coming tomorrow. She liked Debbie. The girl had a spark. She kept it under a bushel most of the time, but Louise Bruning could spot it. She would like to fan the little spark. She thought it would be a good idea to set the bushel on fire and burn it right up. The world had enough sheep in it already.

The three of them would get the house back in shape, she decided. She knew she had let things go, and they couldn't do it all, but they could show her children that she could still manage.

Having a plan made her feel better. She reached for the *Reader's Digest* again, then decided against it. Instead she picked up a book someone had given her that, from what she could gather, was about a seagull who was some kind of a deep thinker. It worked even better than the *Reader's Digest*. She didn't finish two pages before her eyes closed. Soft, warm sleep welcomed her in at last. Dawn was only a couple of hours away, and it wasn't going to be enough, but she would have to take what she could get.

When Peter came down, barefoot, into his grandmother's kitchen, the bottom half of a girl was sticking out from under the kitchen sink. He was pretty sure it was a girl. He blinked, then yawned. They were girl legs, and girl tennis shoes. She was doing something under there. As he waited for this to make sense, the rest of the girl worked her way out and stood up. She had a tool in one hand, some weird type of wrench, and when she saw Peter she froze, like a startled bunny. He couldn't help smiling.

"Sorry," he said. "I didn't mean to scare you. I'm—this is my grandmother's house. I'm Peter. Or Pete. Peter."

She said, "Oh." Then she said, "Hi."

She looked uncertain. Maybe she couldn't decide what her name was, either. The startled bunny expression had given way to a blush.

"You must be 'The Debbie Girl,'" he said.

She nodded and said, "Uh-huh."

"Grosi told me you were coming," he said. "What is that thing, anyway? What were you doing under there?"

"It's a basin wrench," said Debbie. "The faucet was dripping."

She was glad to have something specific to say.

"Wow," said Peter. "You know how to fix that?"

"I think so," she said. "I helped my dad do it once." She was still blushing. She was a blusher. A shy blusher. Peter decided to keep asking her questions.

"Where's my grandmother?" he asked. "Is she awake yet?"

"No," said Debbie. "I'm kind of surprised. She usually is, by this time."

"Oh, good," he said. "That means I can eat breakfast before she puts me to work."

He started poking around in the cupboards. He opened the refrigerator and stood there with the door open. Debbie had returned to her plumbing job. She was turning the faucet on and off and watching it.

"I could have toast with jam," he said. "If I could find some bread. Or I could have cereal, if I could find some milk."

He hadn't considered the possibility that he might starve here. Where, oh where, were the foods of yesteryear? Or even last night? The cupboard was bare. He saw a small bowl of chilled mashed potatoes from last night's dinner and another that held what was left of the cooked cabbage. There was a cluster of bottles that he supposed were medicine of some kind. He wondered how cereal would taste with Cremora. If he added some water, maybe.

"Where does she hide the food?" he asked.

"There isn't a lot," said Debbie. "I don't think she eats very much. She eats a lot of jelly sandwiches."

"That sounds good," said Peter hopefully. It didn't sound good long term, but it would do for right now. "Where's the bread?"

Debbie produced it from a metal box on the counter, and Peter discovered that a ceramic pitcher in the refrigerator had orange juice in it. He made three jelly sandwiches. It being ten o'clock. More like brunch time. He was just tucking into his meal when his grandmother entered the room.

She moved slowly and unsteadily, and she seemed unsettled to find people in her kitchen. She looked from one of them to the other and back, as if she were trying to figure something out.

"Morning, Grosi," said Peter pleasantly. He added, "Hot enough for you?" because he noticed that she was perspiring. Her face was shiny with moisture. It didn't feel all that hot to him, but it was probably something, another thing, about being old. Hot weather was probably harder to take.

His grandmother looked at him, or through him, and muttered something. She sounded angry. It almost sounded like she was cursing at him, though he couldn't be sure because her speech was unclear. And she was speaking in German. He recognized *Dummkopf.* He stopped chewing, puzzled, and saw as she turned away from him that she was going to lose her balance. She might have fallen to the floor, but Debbie and Peter rushed to her, one from each side, and helped her into a chair. The skin of her arms felt damp and clammy.

Their eyes met over her head.

Peter's eyes asked, What is happening?

Debbie's eyes said, I don't know. Something weird.

Peter sat down next to his grandmother.

"Are you feeling okay, Grosi?" he asked.

She didn't answer at first, then she mumbled a few words, but again in German. To Peter's surprise, Debbie responded to her, also in German. She seemed to be asking his grandmother questions. When Grosi tried to answer, her voice was weak and upset.

Peter felt helpless. He couldn't tell if what was happening was a big or a small thing. He looked at Grosi and at Debbie, searching for a clue. Debbie appeared to be thinking. Which she was. She was thinking about a recent episode of *Like Ships in the Night*. Also about the small bottles of insulin inside the door of Mrs. Bruning's refrigerator.

Mrs. Bruning was diabetic. So was Ridge's father, Cliff, on *Like Ships in the Night*. Debbie didn't have the first idea of whether or how to administer insulin, but when Cliff had exhibited these same symptoms on the show, Ridge had saved Cliff's life by dumping some sugar into a glass of orange juice and making him drink it. Cliff had missed eating his breakfast, just like Mrs. Bruning had. That's what Debbie had been asking her. "Did you have any breakfast?" To which Mrs. Bruning had responded, "I keep telling you, I'm not hungry. Nincompoop."

Debbie didn't know if the sugar in the orange juice was a real thing to do, or something made up for TV. She didn't think they could show it on television if it were completely made up.

Peter watched her as she took the lid from the sugar bowl, poured sugar into his orange juice, and fed it to his grandmother, saying more German words. Explaining something. In moments Grosi had revived somewhat. Immediately she started to insist that she was fine. She seemed more herself, but she didn't look fine.

Debbie told his grandmother she was going to use the phone. In English, then German. Debbie went to the phone and put the receiver to her ear.

She listened, she jiggled the silver hook, and listened again. She picked up an envelope from the counter and looked at it. Through the glassine window, she could see today's date, and a notice in red letters. Mrs. Bruning hadn't paid her phone bill. The line was dead.

The neighbors weren't at home. The neighbors' neighbors weren't at home, either. The street was deserted. It would have been a great day for breaking and entering, thought Peter. He ran from house to house, banging on doors, shouting hello, peering through windows, going around from the fronts to the backs. He began trying the doors to see if they were unlocked, thinking he could go in and use the phone. He was surprised at how locked they all were. Where was small town America when you needed it?

Debbie moved between Mrs. Bruning and the back door, the door Peter had gone through, running, to get help. What was taking him so long?

Finally he returned, breathless.

"I can't find anyone who's home," he said. "I've been up and down the street. There's no one anywhere. It's like *Invasion of the Body Snatchers*."

Drifting strains of trumpets and tympani bounced into the yard and floated past the screen door, and Debbie remembered that it was Seldem Days. Everyone was at the parade. Then her eyes fell on a set of keys hanging from a key rack. Car keys.

"Can you drive?" she asked Peter.

"No," he said. "I get my permit next month, though. Then I—" He stopped abruptly as he realized she wasn't saying it to make conversation.

Mrs. Bruning needed to see a doctor. Debbie didn't know how soon, but she thought it had to be soon. Ridge had taken Cliff immediately to the hospital where, unfortunately, Cliff's beautiful young ex-wife, with whom he was still in love, was on duty, and he had a heart attack.

Debbie's mind raced. The hospital itself was too

far away. Two towns away. But it was a straight line, almost, to the fire station. That's where the ambulance was, and someone would be there. Prospect Hill Road, like Pine Street, should be empty.

"Okay," she said. "I guess I will, then."

Peter looked at her. "Do you know how to drive?" he asked.

"Sort of," she said. "Enough to get to the fire station. I just have to check something."

She ran over to the garage and disappeared through the side door. She needed to find out whether Mrs. Bruning's car had a stick shift. It did. That was good, because she didn't know how to do the other kind.

Peter waited for her on the shady porch.

"This is bizarre," he said aloud.

He looked at his watch. Only forty minutes ago he had been sound asleep. Now he found himself stranded, thousands of miles from home, in this backyard that felt both familiar and foreign, alone with a grandmother he didn't know all that well. A grandmother who was suddenly frail and ill, and in need of help.

He wasn't alone, though. He watched Debbie as she ran the short distance back to the house, pushing a sunbleached strand of hair behind her ear, just like Julie Christie. She seemed to know how to do things. All kinds of things. In the current situation Peter found that appealing. He found himself thinking that she would be an interesting girl to hang out with. Maybe they could hop freight trains or depose dictators or something.

"Okay," she said, reaching the patio. "We just have to get her out to the car."

She wasn't even aware that she was smiling, a small, enigmatic smile. It was a reflex action. It was enigmatic because her mind was busy freaking out at what was happening, at what she was about to do. What if it was really stupid to do it—what if Mrs. Bruning really was fine? Maybe they should wait half an hour and see if she felt better.

But when the two of them went back into the kitchen, she was fairly sure that Mrs. Bruning was not fine.

She pressed in the clutch and turned the key, but nothing happened. No engine, no radio, nothing. She tried it again. Still nothing. And nothing once more. She tried to think whether she was forgetting something, but she didn't think so.

"The battery," she said, suddenly remembering Lenny's dad's truck. "Maybe the battery's dead."

She looked around the dark garage as if it might tell her what to do, then over her shoulder at Mrs. Bruning, pale and spent from their journey to the car. Through the rear window, the bright opening of the garage doorway buzzed with leafy green summer life, oblivious to them. The driveway dropped off almost immediately and sloped down to the street. It wasn't a long hill. But it might be enough.

"I think we have to try to pop the clutch," she said.

"Do we know how to do that?" asked Peter.

"We have to push it," said Debbie. "I can help you at first, but as soon as it gets close to the hill, I have to jump in. I'll wait for you at the bottom."

She was sure there was some other really sensible thing they should do instead. But she didn't know what it was.

"Let's just try it," she said. She thought she could do it if she didn't think about it too much.

The car felt even heavier than she had expected. It was monolithic. It wasn't budging. Instinctively she turned around, sat on the front bumper, and put her feet against the wall.

"Okay," she said. "Now try."

After three times there was a slight movement, but the car moved instantly back into place.

"Do it again," said Peter. "Rock it back and forth."

Each time they pushed, the car went back a tiny bit farther, until finally it broke free of the rocking movement and began to roll, just a little, without rolling back.

"Keep going," said Peter. "It's moving."

Debbie pushed against the wall with her feet until her legs were straight and the tips of her toes could no longer reach. She slipped from the bumper onto the gritty garage floor, then scrambled to her feet, ran for the car, jumped in, and gave the engine some gas. The car was rolling, it was rolling backward down the hill, but the engine wasn't starting. She didn't know if she should step on the brake, if that would mess up the procedure.

The car was veering to the left; she overcorrected and went rolling out into the front yard. She overcorrected again, the other way, and zigzagged into the neighbors' yard. And still nothing was happening. Her face was hot, her skin was hot all over, and she felt trembly. This had been a really huge mistake. It was going to be a disaster. But she could stop the car. She could always just stop.

She tried the gas one more time. A little touch. Just a little, little touch. And just as the car rolled over the sidewalk, over the patch of grass and the curb, thunk, down onto the street, the engine turned over and came to life. She stepped on the clutch and shifted into neutral. She put on the brakes, then gave the engine a little more gas. It was running. Debbie was sweating. Her heart was pounding. She realized she was holding her breath, and she let it out.

"Keep breathing," she said to herself. She looked back at Mrs. Bruning, who she had momentarily forgotten all about. Her eyes were, amazingly, or maybe frighteningly, still closed. Debbie saw her chest rise and fall. And again.

Peter Bruning was running down the driveway toward the car. His blond hair flopping, his wire rims glinting, a big grin on his face.

"That was exciting," he said as he jumped inside. "Are you sure you can get us to the fire station? I mean, in one piece and everything?"

He was teasing her. Normally color might have risen to her cheeks, but her circulatory system was completely discombobulated by events and threw up its hands. Rose-colored blotches blossomed and faded in random arrangements on her skin. The back of her arms blushed, and her kneecaps. Her throat, and one of her shins.

"I do better when the engine's running," she said.

It was true. She drove the old car to the fire station with as much concentration as if she were guiding a fat piece of thread through a skinny needle. Slightly but not much faster than that. When they arrived, she said to Peter, "Can you slide over and, if anyone asks, we'll say you drove the car? I'll go in and get someone to help."

"Why?" asked Peter.

"Because we need help. That's why we're here," she said. She couldn't believe he was asking such an obvious question.

"No. I mean, why do you want to say I drove?"

"If my mother finds out I drove a car, she'll kill me," said Debbie. "I don't even have a permit yet. I'm not supposed to know how."

But instead of sliding over, Peter got up on his

knees, turned around, and looked back at his grandmother. He wanted to do something for her, but he didn't know what he should do.

He decided that holding one of her hands would be something good. He took it in his own left hand and covered it with his right. Then he put both of his hands beneath her hand and sort of massaged the top gently with his thumbs. It felt clammy, boney, and limp, but he persevered. He tried to remember the German words Debbie had said to her. There was a good chance, he thought, that if he spoke the words as he remembered them, they would come out either as nonsense syllables or as one of those embarrassing or insulting mistakes you heard about, like when you think you're saying, "What a delicious cake" and what you're really saying is, "Your mother is a dairy cow." He didn't know what she had said, anyway. It might have been, "Your telephone isn't working." That wouldn't be very comforting.

"I love you, Grosi," he said softly. "You're going to be okay."

"Meine Hand, die du da druckst, ist nicht ein Klumpen Brotteig," she murmured back to him. *"Du Schwachkopf."**

He was pretty sure she was speaking affectionately. He was pretty sure she had called him her little dumpling, something like that.

At the hospital they told what had happened over and over. To the admissions clerk, to doctors, nurses, Peter's parents, aunts and uncles, to anyone who asked. They left out the part about the car. It was amazing how easy it was to leave it out. No one asked, everyone assumed the ambulance had come to the house. By the time the doctors had decided that Mrs. Bruning should stay at the hospital for a few days, she had stabilized back to her normal cranky, belligerent self. But when she overheard one of them telling Peter's father that ornery behavior was one of the symptoms of her illness, she immediately shut up

*"That is my hand you are kneading, not a lump of bread dough. Nincompoop."

and retreated to being silently imperious. Which she was very good at. She was the champion.

Once the urgency of the day had subsided, Debbie began to want to get out of there and get home, somehow. Out of the tiny half-room packed with Brunings. She leaned up against the windowsill, trying to make herself small, and looked at the parking lot below. She was thinking she would call and see if anyone was at home who could come and get her, when she saw the Seldem ambulance arriving again, its light flashing. Dave the driver and Jim the other guy hopped out and headed for the back.

She eased her way around Mrs. Bruning's bed as inconspicuously as she could, which was not very, and told Peter, who had ended up on the other side, that Dave was downstairs and she was going to ask if he would give her a ride back to Seldem.

"Me, too," he said. "There's way too many of us in here."

So they did.

∞

It turned out that Mrs. Bruning's car had not been driven long enough to charge the battery. It was dead again.

"I don't know how to do this," whispered Debbie, waiting in the car for Dave to return with jumper cables.

"It's okay," Peter whispered back. "He'll tell you what to do."

Debbie's emergency adrenalin action self was giving way to her don't-get-in-trouble self.

"What if he notices that I don't know what I'm doing?" she said. "What if someone sees me?"

Peter looked at her face to see if she was serious. She was. After all that had happened that day, he thought it was funny that she would worry about this. He spotted a pair of sunglasses in the visor and he set them on Debbie's nose, in front of her own glasses.

"Here," he said. "This can be your disguise. No one will recognize you now." He adjusted the earpieces behind her ears, lifting out the sun-lightened strands of hair that had been trapped beneath them. His fingertips lightly and unintentionally grazed her face and her ears, and Debbie's don't-get-in-trouble self felt itself making room for her alert-alert-something-new-is-happening self. But then Dave returned and signaled to her to release the hood, and she had to stop tingling. Mostly.

"Pay attention," said Peter, leaning toward her. (alert, alert) "This is a skill you need to have if you're going to steal people's cars and save their lives."

"That's not who I am," said Debbie. "I don't do things like this."

"Yes, you do," Peter said. "You do them all the time."

Back at Mrs. Bruning's house, they brought in the mail and the newspaper. Peter washed the dish, butter knife, and juice glass he had used for breakfast while Debbie wiped the counter and put away the bread and the jar of jelly. It was late afternoon. Evening, really. She ought to head home. Still, she looked around for something else to tend to or tidy up.

"My parents are going to stay here while my grandma is in the hospital," said Peter. "Because it's closer for them to visit her from here. I'll go, too, sometimes, but I'm thinking sometimes I'll just stay here and work on her house, like I was going to anyway. Do you think you could come by and—you wouldn't have to actually help, but you could show me where things are, maybe?"

"I can help," said Debbie.

CHAPTER 25
Meanwhile

Down at Seldem Day(s), chicken dinners were being served up by the truckload. It had been a busy day, starting off with the parade in the morning and moving right on through with the sidewalk sale, the slo-pitch tournament, the Miss Seldem pageant, and every other event anyone thought up and was willing to organize.

The "History of Seldem" musical revue was popular. Significant historical events were paired up with musical offerings from local performers. A brief account, for example, of the construction of the power plant down by the river was complemented by a performance of "Smoke on the Water" by Billy Novick's garage band. The arrival of the A&P grocery store was accompanied by the cast of the high school's spring production of *Oliver!* singing "Food, Glorious Food."

Rowanne was in the *Oliver!* number, and Hector watched her from behind the rows of folding chairs. He was also scanning the crowd, still looking for Meadow, but without expecting to find her. He had been looking for her all day as he walked around with Lenny, Patty, and Phil. A couple of times he was sure he had seen her from behind, her dark, curly mop of hair, but each time it was another girl who turned around. A girl who had the dark cloud of hair, but not the dancing stars in her eyes.

He had mentioned Meadow to Phil. But little by little, the hope that she would be there turned into the feeling that she might not, and then the almost-certainty that she wasn't coming. He wasn't that surprised, really. Seldem Days would probably seem dumb if you weren't from Seldem. It was dumb even if you were from Seldem. It was something he could make a joke about next time he saw her. Once he decided she wasn't coming after all, Hector's attention shifted to the festival events and his friends, and he started to enjoy himself.

He and Patty danced several athletic polkas under the big tent set up on the tennis court, to the music of Jimmy's Polka Bandits. Phil and Lenny stayed over on the sidelines, shifting their weight from side to side or leaning back on the cyclone fence. You could tell just by looking that they had no intention of stepping out on the dance floor.

It was beyond Hector how anyone could hear this music without dancing. He had to count out loud to get it right, but he knew a few turns, and now he picked up a couple of new moves from watching the more experienced polka-ers spinning around them.

When the "Twirl Your Hankie Polka" was announced, he and Patty cast wildly about for something to employ as a hankie. Lenny loped over and pulled a folded cotton print bandana from his pocket.

"But we both need one," said Patty.

Lenny smiled his funny little grin, tore an edge of the cloth with his teeth and ripped it into two pieces. He did this with an air of gallantry, and Patty and Hector were briefly impressed until the music started up and they had to dance or be trampled.

It was a minor miracle that Patty danced through the entire set of polka music without falling from or tripping in the platform sandals she had finally persuaded her mother to buy for her. But as they left the tennis court and stepped onto the grass, her foot came down and then down farther, into a rabbit hole. She tipped over and fell, letting out a yelp. The three boys helped her up and supported her, hopping, to the nearest bench, where they decided to wait a few minutes to see if her injury was temporary or more serious.

They happened to be not far from a booth where the Kiwanis Club was selling elephant ears, immense pinwheels of fried pastry coated in sugar, and cups of lemonade. Healing foods, thought Hector. He went over, bought one of each and started back. It was his intention to split the large pastry four ways, but he couldn't resist first just taking a warm sugary bite from what was going to be his quadrant. As he did so, a familiar voice, coming from his left, said, "Whoa, Hector, better watch it. Those things can make you fat, you know."

He turned and saw Dan Persik's face.

And he saw Meadow, smiling her summer day smile as if Dan had said something that was actually funny.

He saw that they were holding hands. Also in his montage of awarenesses, he imagined how he must look, all sweated up from dancing and with a pastry the size of a hubcap dangling from his solitary mouth. He thought of how he disliked Dan Persik. And how he liked Meadow, a lot. He remembered how Meadow had said, "We'll probably come." He had assumed "we" meant Meadow and her cousin

Robin. Did "we" mean Meadow and Dan Persik? Were they already a "we"?

Hector chewed his bite and swallowed it, because he had already bitten it off and there was nothing else he could do. He didn't taste it. Swallowing without saliva was difficult. The doughy lump lodged in his throat. A sip of lemonade moved it only a fraction of an inch.

Continuing with his stupid joke, Dan Persik said, "Yeah, those things are full of calories."

That's a big word for you, isn't it? thought Hector. Then he said, "Thanks for the tip. I'll have to remember that from now on."

And in some kind of a grand impulsive gesture, he tossed the elephant ear away as if it were a Frisbee. He didn't even look to see where he was tossing it. He didn't care.

But when he heard someone say, "Oof," and saw Meadow's eyes widen, he stole a quick peek. The elephant ear lay broken in the grass, at the feet of an elderly woman who was gingerly rubbing her throat and brushing sugar from the bodice of her dress.

"Score," said Dan.

Hector watched from the corner of his eye as she looked around, said something to her husband, and moved on.

God, he thought. I could have killed her. Remorse and humiliation saturated the already existing lousiness of the situation. The only positive feeling he felt was a grain of relief, a huge grain, but still just a grain, that the old lady was okay. He glanced back at her to make sure she was still walking. She was.

What a complete and total idiot I am, he thought. What an ass.

He was still standing in a conversational grouping with Dan and Meadow. He had no idea what to do next.

"On the other hand, I think I'd better postpone my new diet," he said. "It could be dangerous to other people's health."

And he exited, stage right.

245

Phil, just two yards away on the bench, had seen and heard it all as it happened. Hector sat down beside him.

"What an idiot," Hector said. During his short walk to the bench, he had transferred the mantle of stupidity to the broad shoulders of Dan Persik. He had to do it. He could beat himself up later.

" 'Better watch out, Hector. Those things make you fat.' He can't even insult me in an original way."

"You should have said, 'At least my fat isn't all in my head,' " suggested Phil, who had been thinking about it.

"I should have said—I don't even know what I should have said. His stupidness is contagious. It's like a disease. A cloud of contagion that infects everyone around him. That must be why girls drool all over him; they become stupid and they can't help themselves."

"Girls drool over him because he's a hunk," said Patty, joining in the discussion.

"A hunk of what?" said Hector. "What is so great about being big and strong and stupid?"

"And handsome," added Patty. "Big, strong, stupid, and handsome."

"What is so great about that?" asked Hector.

"Gee, I don't know," said Patty. Just a little sarcastically. "I guess it wouldn't be anything like being pretty and twinkly and looking good in a halter top. Or having a nice tan—hey, there's a reason to like someone."

Hector saw what she was getting at, but he didn't think it applied. He liked Meadow for her inner beauty. Which happened, in her case, to be accompanied by outer beauty. He thought her outer beauty might even be a result of her inner beauty. A time-honored line of reasoning that encompasses both truth and quicksand. He hoped his own inner self was somehow visible from the outside. It had to be, somehow.

"I'm a hunk in my soul," he said.

"A hunk of what?" said Lenny.

"Fried dough," said Hector. "Smothered in sugar." It was an easy joke.

Then he added, "Faster than a speeding bullet. More powerful than a locomotive. Able to wipe out old ladies in a single throw."

I'm a cartoon, he thought. My life is a cartoon.

Patty and Phil smiled, Lenny guffawed. They could see that steam was still coming out of Hector's ears. Lenny asked Patty how her ankle was feeling. He helped her up and she leaned on his arm for support while she hobbled in a circle, carefully testing her injured leg.

Phil, watching them, said quietly to his friend, "You can make all the jokes you want, but that was her, right? And she's here with that moron."

Hector nodded as he found a sugary crumb on

his face near his mouth, looked at it on his fingertip, and touched it to his tongue, where it dissolved in a brief sweetness.

Dan Persik and Meadow moved on through the fair.

Now and then Hector saw them go here and go there. When he did, he averted his eyes. But they would go back, just for a few seconds, the way fingertips return involuntarily to a wound to see if it still hurts, to find out whether it feels any different than it did a minute ago. It felt the same each time he checked.

Dan and Meadow were having a good time. They weren't doing it to spite anyone. It's just fun to be a healthy beautiful young person walking around on a sunny afternoon with another healthy beautiful young person. A lot of fun. They shared their golden selves with the world, and the world smiled back.

The warm apple dumpling booth stopped Dan in his tracks.

"Whoa," he said. He said "whoa" a lot. Or maybe it was "Wo."

"I have to have one of these. They're amazing. Have you ever had one?"

"No," said Meadow. "But I don't think I can eat anything else for a little while."

"I'm not really hungry, either," said Dan. "But these are so good. And if I don't eat one now, I have to wait a whole year.

"I have dreams about these," he said to the three grandmotherly women who were serving. They cackled merrily. One of them handed him his paper plate, already capsizing with warm, soggy dumpling. Another said, "They do seem to have a powerful effect on people." The third called out, "Enjoy!"

"I think I have to sit down to eat this," said Dan. "It's leaking all over the place."

They scanned the picnic tables for an opening, spotted one, and made their way toward it. The only people sitting at the table were Russell Kebbesward and his little sister, Annette. Russell was in a band uniform; Annette was still dressed as a ragamuffin orphan. She had been in the "Food, Glorious Food" number.

Meadow greeted them and asked if Annette was Russell's sister. There was a resemblance. She noticed Annette's costume, and the two girls fell into a conversation about the history play, and then about *Oliver!* Watching Dan eat had been entertaining for a while, but Meadow was beginning to get a little bored with it.

Dan was immersed in the perfection of his dumpling. The tartness of the apple, mellowed and softened by baking; the hot, gooey cinnamon-sugary apple juices inside the tender flaky crust; the melting ice cream . . . he scarfed it down. And then, too late, his stomach reminded him of what was already down in there: Hot dogs. Chicken. French fries. Corn on the cob.

His stomach's burgeoning size crowded his heart, especially the underdeveloped kindness lobe. He felt annoyed that Meadow was talking to Annette. Annoyed that he was sitting with Russell Kebbesward.

Russell was trying to eat a chicken dinner without getting grease on his band uniform. He thought he should say something friendly to Dan. Meadow had been friendly when they sat down, and Dan had made a grunting noise that might have been friendly. Now Meadow and Annette were talking. He thought he should say something to Dan. Now that they were in the same guitar class and everything.

"Have you been practicing your guitar?" he asked.

"Huh?" said Dan, when he realized Russell had spoken to him.

"Have you been practicing your guitar?" Russell repeated.

Dan looked at him, briefly, as if Russell were a rock he had stubbed his toe on. Then he reached across the table, gently put his hand on Meadow's arm, and said, "I'm done. Let's go."

There was a barely perceptible subdermal movement near his tailbone. There was a slight bray in his voice.

It was all still reversible.

Later, sitting in the grass waiting for the fireworks to get started, Hector absentmindedly pulled up a daisy and began picking the white petals off, one by one. Whatever natural light was left to the day had retreated to the daisies scattered in the dark grass and to white shirts sprinkled through the crowd. He pulled the petals off till they were gone, and all that was left was the yellow-gold circle, dimmer than the white, but still visible.

It was funny, he thought, how up until you pulled the last petal off, it was beautiful. A symbol of love. But once your fortune was told, it didn't remind anyone of love anymore and it wasn't beautiful. It was a mutilated flower. A deflowered flower. Something to throw away. He yanked up another one and did it again. *She loves me, she loves me*

254

not. The words said themselves automatically in his head. Halfway around, he changed the words to *she loves me not, she loves me not, she loves me not, she loves me not, she loves me not, she loves me not, she loves me not, she loves me not, she loves me not, she loves me not, she loves me not.* There. The perfect emblem for him. He slid it into a buttonhole of his shirt.

Despite his mood, he couldn't help noticing a catchy rhythm going through his brain. When he paid attention, he heard the words that ran through it:

> she loves me not,
> she loves me,
> she loves me not,
> she loves me,
> she loves me not, she loves me not, she loves
>   me not,
> she loves me
> not.

The faint voice in his head was singing with a

Caribbean accent. The rhythm had maracas, it might be calypso. Or a samba. Something Latin, he really didn't know. He tried to hear the melody, to guess what the chords might be. He was thinking A—D—A.

A—D—A—something.

CHAPTER 26
Somewhere Else

What they decided was to go to the bus station, get on the first bus that came through, and get off at the next place it stopped, no matter where it was. They would spend a few hours there, then come back. It was an experiment.

They thought of it while they were excavating last autumn's rotting dead leaves and maybe the rotting dead leaves from the year before that from Mrs. Bruning's deep window wells so there would be room for this year's dead leaves. They were talking about Seldem versus California. Debbie thought California had to be better. More interesting.

"It has to be," she said, raking the leaves over to join the ivy they had pulled away from the downstairs windows.

"Not necessarily," said Peter. "You can be bored or interested anywhere. I get bored in California. But it *is* interesting to go someplace else. I really like how when you go somewhere for the first time, everything seems unusual. Should we do the gutters next?"

"We probably should," said Debbie. "Hold on a second and I'll help you with the ladder."

She finished herding her pile up to the growing biomass and set down her rake.

"There's nothing unusual here," she said. "It's very usual."

"Not to me," said Peter.

"Name one thing," said Debbie. "One unusual thing."

"Okay," said Peter. He thought for a minute. "People here say 'yinz.'"

"That's not how you say it," said Debbie. "It's 'y'ns.' Almost like there's no vowel. Or it can be like in 'book.' Not everyone says it, though. I don't. You think that's interesting?"

"Kind of," said Peter. "I've never heard people say it anywhere else. There are other things that are probably more interesting. That's just an easy one to point out."

They had propped the ladder against the old house, and he climbed up to empty the gutters. Fistfuls of decomposing vegetable matter started dropping to the ground like slime bombs. Debbie stepped out of the way. She could rake them up when Peter moved on to the next section.

A few minutes later he said, "Okay, I have one. People here build houses on hillsides that are practically vertical. They're like cliff dwellers. And there's this gas station between my aunt's house and here that's sort of built into the base of a hill that was cut away for the road to go through. It's made of stone, too, so it looks like it's part of the cliff, and it looks old, like an archaeological ruin. But there's a Sinclair sign on it, and pumps out front, and it has windows, and tires piled up on the side. It's like you're filling up your tanks at Stonehenge, or Machu Picchu."

Debbie knew exactly what kind of places he was talking about, and she thought they were interesting, too. But they weren't in Seldem. They were still Somewhere Else.

"I wonder how far from where you live you have to go," she said, "before it gets interesting."

"I don't think you have to go very far at all," said Peter. "I mean, think about it. You just go to someone's house for the first time, and it's different. Not always, but it can be."

"So, if you went to another town, even nearby, it might be even more different."

"Maybe the same amount of difference," said Peter. "It could be interesting, though. It could be fun."

"You could go on the bus," said Debbie.

"Where?" asked Peter. He was climbing back up now.

"I don't know," said Debbie. "Anywhere. You could just get on a bus, the first bus that shows up, and get off somewhere. The first stop."

She said it hypothetically. She said hypothetical things all the time. In theory, she was the adventurous type.

Peter didn't know about the hypotheticalness of Debbie's life. He thought it was a brilliant idea that should be acted on. And he was ready for a break from his grandmother's rotting house.

"Let's do it," he said. "Let's do it tomorrow."

So they did.

As they studied the bus schedule taped to the window of Jim's Bargain Store, which also happened to be the bus station, Debbie noticed that all of the buses heading north stopped to pick up passengers in Birdvale, and that the ones going south stopped in Hesmont.

"I think we need to go farther than one stop," she said. "I go to those places all the time."

They decided that half an hour would be about the right amount of time to spend on the bus and, checking the timetable again, they picked the town of New Bridge.

"Have you been there?" asked Peter.

"We drive through it on our way to other places," said Debbie. "But I've never walked around in it."

"Let's go there, then," said Peter.

Even Birdvale looked different when you were passing through it on a bus. Before there was time to think about why, it was gone, and other scenes went flashing by the window. The close-up scenes flashed by; the backgrounds moved more slowly. Fast and close included John and Jerry's Fruit Market, River Sand and Supply, the row of company houses just before the Blentz Bridge. Slower: the islands in the river. The rooftops and smokestacks of the air brake factory on the other side. The sky.

In New Bridge they stepped from the bus and

found themselves standing in front of a bakery. Warm, sweet bakery aromas filled the morning air; the window under the striped awning was stacked with golden brown loaves and rolls and cakes on pedestals.

"This is a good omen," said Peter.

As the bus pulled away behind them, it exhaled a hot, choking blast of exhaust that temporarily overpowered the bakery smells. But the noxious cloud didn't last. The bakery smells won out.

Inside they chose an unsliced loaf of Italian bread and a quart of chocolate milk. It was Peter's idea. On her own Debbie would have picked out a cookie or a doughnut, maybe a cream puff or an eclair, some individual serving type of treat. But she immediately saw the appeal of ripping hunks of bread from a shared, still-warm loaf.

The street outside the bakery didn't look promising for picnic spots. Until, in the space between two buildings, Debbie saw a section of a bridge.

"Look," she said, "I wonder if it's the New Bridge."

Peter's eyes followed hers, and he said, "Hey, should we see if we can go down by the water?"

Debbie thought they should.

So they started off in that direction, making left turns and right turns down narrow, tilting streets in hopes that they would average out to a diagonal. They walked through an old neighborhood of densely built houses. Some of them were separated only by inches.

"I wonder how they did that," said Debbie. "They must have built the second one from the inside."

Peter pointed out a series of mysterious arrows, circles, and numbers spray painted onto the sidewalk.

Debbie thought that the bike chain around the bottom of a tree looked like an ankle bracelet.

They heard a woman's voice yelling from deep inside a house, asking if anyone wanted pancakes and sausages.

Two dogs appeared on the sidewalk ahead of them, silhouetted on the crest of a hill.

The dogs, who looked huge and threatening from a distance, and who still looked huge and threatening from up close, parted around them like the Red Sea.

All along the way, ordinary things became unordinary. The day was full of signs and wonders.

They had almost forgotten that they were headed for the bridge, when there it was. They clambered down over the huge boulders around the piling, then took off their shoes to try to dangle their feet in the water. It was too far down.

Peter turned so that he was facing the rock and lowered himself to his elbows.

"My feet are in, but it's not very relaxing," he said through clenched teeth. He hoisted himself back up and they sat on the rock in the sun, with the crusty bread and the chocolate milk, watching the river go by.

"There's the moon," said Debbie. "It's full."

The moon was a white disc in the daytime sky.

"I wonder," she said, "if you looked at the sky, in summer and in winter, and if you couldn't feel the temperature, and both days were clear-sky days, if you could tell which was which somehow, just by looking. Or if they would look exactly the same. Or instead of the sky, maybe at a rock, in the sunshine. Or the river."

"I bet animals could tell," said Peter. "Certain animals. Or birds. They probably have internal sundials or something, that can register the angle of the sun's rays. But I bet people couldn't."

When they had watched the river for a long enough while, they walked back downtown. Everything was still being interesting.

At some point Peter took Debbie's hand, and held it. Lightly and easily, as if it were no big deal. It was the most interesting thing yet.

Debbie waited for the black hole to take over her brain. When she didn't feel that happening, she stole a peek at Peter's face. Only to find he was looking at hers. Was this possible?

Later, on the bus again, Peter wanted to tell her about a theory he was making up.

"I think," he said, "that it's a good thing to get out of your usual, you know, surroundings. Because you find things out about yourself that you didn't know, or you forgot. And then you go back to your regular life and you're changed, you're a little bit different because you take those new things with you. Like a Hindu, except all in one life: you sort of get reincarnated depending on what happened and what you figure out. And any one place can make you go forward, or backward, or neither, but gradually you find all your pieces, your important pieces, and they stay with you, so that you're your whole self no matter where you go. Your Buddha self. That's my theory, anyway."

He had been reading *Siddhartha*, which he found

in his brother's room. He probably wouldn't have said all of this to anyone he knew at home, and he wondered if he sounded too weird. He didn't need to worry. Debbie had been separated from her moorings and there was a spongy piece of her left open to the universe in whatever form it might take. The form it was taking was him. She thought it was an amazing theory, even though she didn't quite know what he was talking about. But it was the main thing she believed in right now, along with buses and chocolate milk and Italian bread.

Peter was holding her hand again. The bus was moving much too quickly through the afternoon landscape.

"Do you have a theory?" he asked.

Debbie's theory at the moment was that everything was perfect. This day was perfect. The bus was perfect and the world outside was perfect. She had a place in the perfect world, a perfect place, and she was in it. This didn't sound very substantial next to Buddha and Hinduism, so she said, "Not exactly."

"Yes, you do," said Peter. "You have a lot of theories. I can tell. You have theories about everything."

Nothing happened, everything happened. It was a perfect day.

Except that two days later, Peter got on an airplane with his parents. And then he was just gone. Back to California.

Debbie had an address on a scrap of paper in the drawer of her desk. She had an invisible cloud of new feelings that went around with her. Two souvenirs from Somewhere Else. Two pieces of her Buddha puzzle. She didn't have the first idea where to put them.

dead worm song

As I went out this morning, to walk the night away,

To dry the teardrops from my eyes and start a brand-new day,

All night the rain had fallen, and there upon the ground

I saw the sorry earthworms that were half-squished all around.

(refrain) I saw those dead worms, and dying—

Worms that haven't long to be,

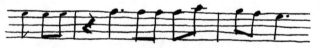

I see those dead worms and I start crying

'cause they re- mind me of your dead love for me. . . .

CHAPTER 27
Meanwhile, Elsewhere

A bus was just pulling away from the curb into traffic as Hector walked past Jim's Bargain Store, and he held off on breathing until he was out of range of its poisonous fumes.

Other than the bus farts, the air was clear and fresh. It had been washed by an overnight rain, which had also flooded many, many worms out of house and home. They were scattered all over the sidewalks, wondering what happened.

Many had already been stepped on.

They didn't have to wonder anymore.

Hector avoided stepping on worms if he could help it, though if you weren't paying attention you could do it without realizing it. He thought you would feel a squish. But maybe you wouldn't.

He made up a song about the worms as he walked along. Not on purpose; it just happened. It was a country song. And it was a stupid song. He didn't care. That's the mood he was in. He was thinking maybe he would specialize in stupid songs. Probably he'd be really good at it.

He made up a verse about being stepped on that was very satisfying. Although he knew that he hadn't actually been stepped on. He hadn't been stepped on, but he still felt he had something in common with the worms.

CHAPTER 28

Mrs. Bruning

When Mrs. Bruning came home, she seemed small. Maybe it was the house that felt bigger. Debbie and Peter had put away or gotten rid of some of the stuff, and it was more spacious.

But she seemed smaller even within her house-dress, and her skin didn't fit as snugly as it had before. Her brown eyes were still bright, though, under her thin white dandelion puff of hair.

The Brunings had hired a visiting nurse to come

and check on her, and they had signed her up for Meals on Wheels. She would never have signed up for it herself, and she didn't like walking able-bodied to the door and accepting food someone else had cooked, but it was part of the deal she had made with her children. And it made a change from having cereal for dinner, or canned soup.

She refused to have the housekeeper. She didn't want some stranger in her house, handling and moving everything. She insisted that, with Debbie's help, she could manage.

Debbie looked around to see if any of the neighbors were at home before going inside Mrs. Bruning's. Once, while she thought Mrs. B. was elsewhere in the house, she picked up the phone in the kitchen to make sure there was a dial tone. Mrs. Bruning saw her listening, then carefully lowering the receiver onto the hook.

"I don't blame you," she said. "I'd check up on me, too."

Mrs. Bruning also noticed that Debbie was going into the living room a lot. When she headed in there again, Mrs. B. waited a minute, then tiptoed after her. She wasn't light on her feet, but she knew where the creaky spots were.

Standing in the shadowy hallway, she saw that Debbie was just dusting. Dusting the pictures on the mantelpiece.

Disappointed, she was about to sneak away again when Debbie did something that surprised her. Then didn't surprise her. Debbie carried one of the framed pictures to a chair and sat down and looked at it. Louise Bruning couldn't see the picture from where she was, but she knew by its size and shape and where it had been sitting that it was a photograph, a couple of years old, of her grandson Peter.

Just for the fun of seeing Debbie jump, she said softly, "I have a newer one. I'll give it to you."

Debbie's reaction was satisfying. She looked up as if she had been caught stealing the silverware.

Then she looked around for her dust rag, which she had left on the mantel. She jumped up and grabbed it and started dusting again.

"Come out to the kitchen," said Mrs. Bruning. "I think that's where I have it, in a drawer in there."

CHAPTER 29
Elephants

Debbie sat cross-legged on her bed, leaning over a photo album. Just beyond the album were the two boxes from the closet.

The photograph of Peter that Mrs. Bruning had given her was propped up against the hatbox in such a way that someone opening the curtain and looking in her room wouldn't see it. The photo album from her mother's college years was opened to several photos of Helen Brandt and her friends posed on skis, laughing, on a sunny, snowy hillside, in swimsuits. All of them wore red lipstick and had wavy hair. They looked glamorous, in an old-fashioned way.

They didn't look like they would ever feel awkward, would ever not know what to say, to a boy or to anyone else.

But photo albums aren't a good place to look if you're wondering about things like that.

Debbie wondered if it was true that there was only one person in the world for every person, and if she had already met him, and she either had to find a way to be around him again someday or always be alone. Romance-wise. She didn't quite believe this. What seemed more likely was that there were at least five or six people scattered around the globe who you could bump into and, wham, it would be the right thing. The odds probably varied from person to person. For Chrisanne there were probably fifty or sixty, all in the continental U.S. Maybe even within the tristate area. Debbie's handful were somewhere in the Himalayas, or the steppes of Russia, or passing her by in a crowd, unsuspecting.

So that if she thought she might have found one of them, she shouldn't just give up. Should she?

Debbie heard footsteps, and she quickly stuffed the picture of Peter down between her bed and the wall. The curtain moved, and her mother's head appeared.

"You have a letter," she said. "From California."

Debbie's heart sprang up and bounded across the room in one jump. The rest of her sat in simulated calmness on her bed. She put an expression of surprised curiosity on her face and said, "I do?"

Her mother handed her the letter and leaned on the doorway, waiting to see what it said. She thought it might be a thank-you note, though it felt thicker.

Debbie opened the envelope and pulled out a letter and a photo. She couldn't help smiling a little; it was the same picture she already had.

She explained to her mother that the letter was from Mrs. Bruning's grandson. The one who had been there the day Mrs. Bruning went to the hospital, the one she had worked with on Mrs. Bruning's house for those few days. She wanted to let her mother know that he was more than that to her, a lot more, so she said offhandedly, "He was really nice. He was fun to be with."

Her mother didn't hear the hidden message, which was, It was amazing and perfect to be with him and now my life seems dull and empty.

Debbie showed her the photo, thinking, this will explain everything; now she will understand. It was a school picture of a boy with chin-length blond hair, parted down the middle and tucked behind his ears. He wore wire-rimmed glasses, a T-shirt, a denim jacket.

So often in books, or in movies, one character looks at another character and understands in a precise way what that person is feeling. So often in real life, one person wants to be understood, but obscures her feelings with completely unrelated words and facial expressions, while the other person is trying to remember whether she did or didn't turn off the burner under the hard-boiled eggs.

Helen did sense something, an undercurrent. She thought that Debbie probably had a crush on this boy. But California was pretty far away, and she couldn't have gotten to know him very well in such a short time. Maybe they would exchange a few letters.

"He looks very nice," she said. "He's a cute boy."

"He is nice," said Debbie.

It was as close as she could come to saying, "I need to go to California. Can I?"

But it wasn't very close, not close enough. Her mother had no way of knowing that this would have been a good time to tell her daughter that she had once known a boy who went away. A boy who had made a game of finding little figures of dogs, and giving them to her. They might have talked then about how that felt, and what you did next. But their secrets inadvertently sidestepped each other, unaware, like blindfolded elephants crossing the tiny room.

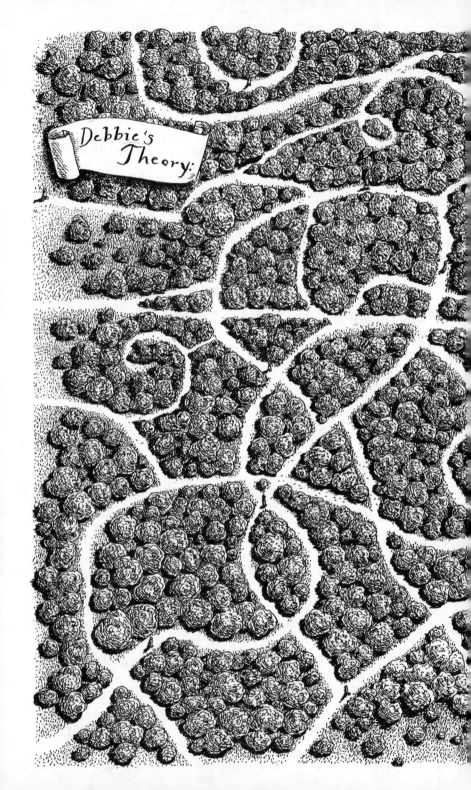

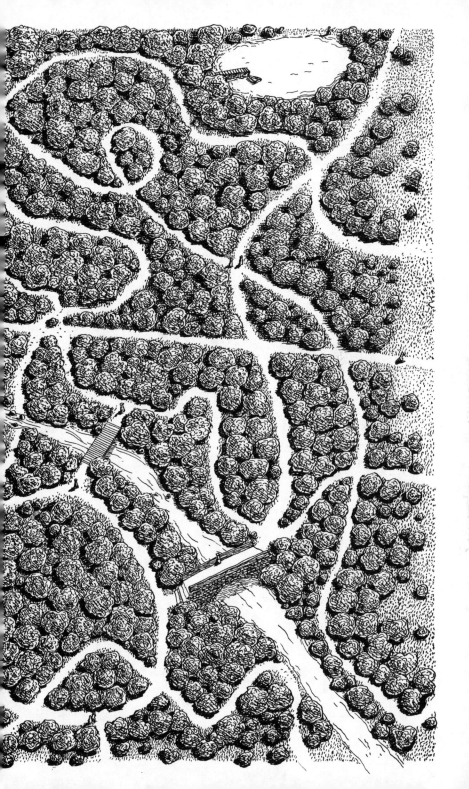

CHAPTER 30

What Patty Said When Debbie Showed Her the Photo

was, "Maybe I could go work for Mrs. Bruning, too."

CHAPTER 31
California of the Mind

Walking around Seldem with a letter in your pocket was different than walking around Seldem with no letter. Debbie stopped to look at a pile of dirt with pipes coming out of it. She didn't know what it was there for, but it looked like at any moment the pipes could organize themselves into the legs of a giant mechanical tarantula and rise up from the dirt.

The old nun at Our Lady of Victory was watering

the roses that grew outside the convent, with a hose. Or rather, she was standing near the roses, playing with the hose. She squeezed the trigger rhythmically, releasing temporary nebulas of droplets that rose together, catching the sunlight in a hundred synchronized sparkles, then fell together and landed on nothing in particular. She seemed to be having a good time.

A little farther on Debbie leaned on an overgrown chain-link fence. A flash of red had caught her eye, and she wanted to see what it was. It was an immense woodpecker, bigger than her forearm, that had flown into a dappled grove of honey locusts. After a minute he flew off. Debbie saw that a tiny creek flowed through the grove and, on an impulse, fished a dime from her pocket, tossed it in, and made a wish. The splash startled a small, furry animal she hadn't noticed, and it scurried into the shadows.

Seldem felt like someone had plugged it in.

Like someone you've always known who has suddenly revealed hidden depths. Not deep dark depths. Just depths. Texture.

But when she returned home, she felt ordinary again. Maybe even less than ordinary. She felt for the letter in her back pocket. It was there, but it might as well have been a grocery list. It wasn't working anymore. Maybe she had used it up.

All evening she felt ordinary. She sat on the couch in the basement feeling ordinary. She went upstairs to take a shower, and when she had undressed, she looked in the mirror. Ordinary, ordinary, less than ordinary. She had taken her glasses off, so she was squinting a little. It made her look mildly fierce. Her hair, usually pulled back, fell to her shoulders in an unbrushed mass, curling and frizzing in the humid air. She frowned at her squinting, frizzing, ordinary reflection. Why did she think something good could happen to her?

But then something did. Something good and

mysterious. It's hard to explain why, but she started to laugh. She laughed at her fierce naked self, frowning into the mirror. And she liked the girl who was laughing.

It was a small piece of her Buddha self, snapping into place.

CHAPTER 32

Dan Persik's Progress

It wasn't the first time Dan Persik had seen the man with the missing legs. But it was the first time he had spoken to him. Dan was sitting on a bench waiting for a bus when the guy came vaulting along the sidewalk. Dan, being an athlete, observed his technique and his equipment, the leather encasement held on by industrial strength suspenders and the gloves. His own practiced muscles imagined performing in this same event. The man without legs arrived at Dan's bench, placed his hands on it, lifted himself up, and turned himself around so he was facing the right way. He obviously had tremendous upper-body strength. Dan admired this, and he respected the guts it took to haul yourself all over town this way.

They greeted each other, then Dan said, "So, what happened to your legs?"

He asked with genuine interest. The man, who introduced himself and shook Dan's hand, found that refreshing. It was a pleasant change from the more frequent reactions of pretending not to notice that he didn't have legs, or ignoring him completely. He didn't blame anyone, but this felt better. He told Dan, briefly, how he had been separated from his legs. It was a war story.

"That sucks," said Dan. What he said was exactly true, and heartfelt. He asked the guy a few questions about how fast he could go, how much ground he covered in a day, how high a surface he could lift himself up to, then their conversation shifted to other topics. Sports. The heat wave.

Dan's bus came. He said, "See you around," and got on.

He had been a decent human being without even trying, or thinking about it. He could do that.

Now, with an equal lack of effort, he handed the

driver a transfer he had found on the sidewalk and took the last available seat. Casting his gaze outside the window, he pretended not to notice the woman with a toddler on her hip who had gotten on behind him.

First come, first served, he thought.

The scales tipped back and forth. It was so hard to tell what he might come back as in another life, or even who he would turn out to be in this one.

CHAPTER 33

A Pig Roast

When Phil mentioned that there was going to be a block party on their street, Hector said, "Hey, maybe I should bring up my guitar and play a few songs."

Phil looked over at his friend and said, "Are you serious?"

"I need to practice playing in front of people," said Hector. "Do you think it would be okay?"

Phil shrugged.

"I guess so," he said. "I don't think anybody

would care. But are you thinking that people will be, like, paying attention, or singing along? Because if it's more than one or two songs, I wouldn't count on it."

"That's okay," said Hector. "I can be background music. Or if it seems really stupid, I can always just stop. Or not do it. What else is going to happen?"

"Nothing," said Phil. "It's just a party, like a picnic, in the middle of the street. They're going to put roadblocks at both ends. We'll drag out everybody's picnic tables and put them all together. The big event of the evening is that Lenny and his dad are going to roast a pig."

"They're going to roast a pig?" echoed Hector.

"A whole pig," said Phil. "They made their own pig roaster."

"A pig roast," said Hector. "So it's going to be kind of like a luau."

"Hnh," said Phil, a sound that was not quite a laugh. It was about one-sixth of a laugh. "Only in that one small way," he said. "In every other way, it won't be anything like a luau."

"I wonder if I have time to learn 'Tiny Bubbles,'" mused Hector. It was the only Hawaiian song he knew, although the only Hawaiian thing about it was that it was sung by a singer named Don Ho, who was from Hawaii.

"I wouldn't go to any trouble," said Phil. He could almost see Hector's brain working.

"It's a great song," said Hector. "I'd want to learn it anyway."

CHAPTER 34

Roasting the Pig

Leon and Lenny had made the pig roaster themselves, out of an old fuel oil tank they found in their basement. In a way, that's how the block party got started, because once you make a pig roaster, you want to try it out, and it takes a lot of people to eat a pig. And a lot of hours to roast one.

They got out of bed at three in the morning and bumped softly down the dim, blurry hallway into the kitchen. Lenny flicked on the light over the sink and they both stood there, frowning and squinting. Leon plugged the cord of the waiting percolator into its waiting wall socket, the red light went right on, and the gurgling started up. It sounded so awake.

Outside in the cool quiet of the night, they started the truck and drove the roaster to a spot on the side of the street that was close to where the party would be, near the streetlight, and where there would be shade most of the day. Leon emptied the bags of charcoal into the bottom of the tank and fussed around getting it to burn, while Lenny lifted down a sawhorse with reflectors nailed onto it and a couple of lawn chairs. They were both trying to be quiet; every bump and scrape seemed to tear holes in the silence. Far off, down by the river, a train blew its whistle and rumbled through town. Another person awake.

"Go see if that coffee is ready and put it in the thermos," said Leon, the first words that had been spoken aloud.

"Okay," said Lenny. He was feeling somewhat alert now.

In the kitchen he poured the coffee into the thermos. He screwed on the lid that was like a plug, then the one that was a cup, and then he thought maybe he would have a cup, too. He took a mug from the cupboard and poured some half-and-half into it. He considered the bowl of sugar cubes and put five cubes in his pocket.

After they got the pig into the roaster, Leon said that Lenny should go back to bed. But Lenny said he wasn't tired. So they sat there in the lawn chairs on the asphalt, just out of the reach of the streetlight. A pleasant warmth radiated from the roaster. They sipped their coffee. Lenny had tasted coffee before, without getting what the big attraction was. He didn't really get it now, either. The warmth of it was nice, though, in the chilly hours before dawn. It felt nice in his hands. The taste was almost tolerable with the half-and-half. He had dropped in one sugar cube, but he hadn't brought anything along to stir it with, so it was dissolving at the bottom of the cup, waiting down there in a soft tasty lump.

Leon smiled to himself as Lenny's head started to bob. Who but a kid could fall asleep sitting up in a lawn chair, drinking coffee? He gently removed the cup from Lenny's hands and set it on the street, then reached into the truck, pulled out a jacket, and draped it carefully around Lenny's shoulders. Lenny's eyelids fluttered, then closed again.

Leon sat back down and poured himself a little more coffee. He was used to being awake in the middle of the night. He liked it. A cricket was chirping, slowly. There was a way of telling the temperature by how far apart the chirps were. Faster chirping meant warmer air, which everyone knew, but it was more precise than that, you could multiply it by some number, he thought, and get the temperature. And locusts, which made a lot of noise, too, but in the daytime, had a seven-year cycle. So you would know seven years had gone by, just in case you weren't keeping track. Or was it seventeen years? He closed his eyes while he tried to remember which it was. It felt good to have his eyes closed, and he forgot to think about it, whatever it was he had been thinking about.

CHAPTER 35
Sarong

The coincidental thing was that Hawaiian music seemed to include guitars. Hector found a picture in a magazine of a luau and there was definitely a guy playing a guitar. The outfit the guy was wearing was pretty wild. He was wearing an ordinary white shirt with a button-down collar. The sleeves were rolled up halfway. But then, instead of pants, he was wearing something that must have been a sarong, of shimmering silk, and then flip-flops. He also wore, of course, a lei of flowers. It was an unexpected combination, the oxford shirt and the sarong, but the more he looked at it, the more authentic it seemed. It looked really good, in fact. Hector had an oxford shirt. He also happened to have a sarong. Or at least he knew where to find one.

"Wait a minute," said Rowanne. "Who said you could use that?"

"Will you help me tie it?"

He showed Rowanne the picture in the magazine.

"I have a gig at a luau," he said. "Actually, it's just a block party, but they're roasting a pig."

"Someone hired you?" she asked.

"Not exactly," he said. "Actually, they don't even know I'm coming. Well, Phil knows. It's on his street."

"I see," said Rowanne. She studied the picture carefully.

They tried several approaches to wrapping her

India-print bedspread around Hector before they came up with an arrangement that both resembled a sarong and would not fall off.

"Your cutoffs are making it lumpy."

"I'm not taking off my cutoffs," said Hector.

"Well, can you at least take your wallet out of your pocket?"

"The shirt hangs over that part anyway; it won't show. Can I borrow your flip-flops?"

When Hector put on his shirt and slung the guitar over his shoulder, he and Rowanne were both surprised at how well he had turned out. The fabric was bunched up in some uncomfortable places that made him think that the Hawaiian guys must do it a little differently, but visually it had the right effect.

"It would be even better if I had a lei," he said.

"Oh, well," said Rowanne. "You have nice calves," she observed. "No, really," she said, when he looked to see if she was being sarcastic. "It's interesting. I don't know why, but wearing a skirt makes your legs suddenly seem very masculine. Too bad you don't live in Hawaii. Because except for this special occasion, I don't think you could pull it off here."

In light of that thought, she added, "Do you want a ride?"

"It's only a fifteen-minute walk."

"Fifteen minutes in Seldem in a sarong?"

Hector wasn't worried about walking around Seldem in a sarong. He had always been able to get away with things. The flip side was that no one took him seriously. But he wasn't worried about that right now, either.

"It's okay," he said. "I can do it. But can you pick me up later? Like at ten-thirty or eleven? Unless I call earlier."

CHAPTER 36

Flip-Flop, Necklace

Hector ran across the street to beat a car that was coming down the hill. It was a stupid thing to do in a sarong and flip-flops carrying a guitar case, especially when he was not even used to walking in flip-flops. He should have waited, but oh, well. One of the flip-flops came off and he had to finish crossing with one off and one on and wait for the car to pass. It drove right over the flip-flop, but the flip-flop was resilient. A little soiled, but still springy. When he picked it up, he saw something that had not been so lucky. A gold necklace lay flattened, embedded in a patch of tar.

No cars were coming just then, and he picked at a part of the necklace with his fingernail until it lifted free. As he gently tugged the rest of it up, it left behind a precise impression of itself. He carried it with him back to the sidewalk and took a closer look.

The chain seemed to be okay, but the catch was broken and the middle was damaged. It had several little hooked-together pieces, letters maybe, that seemed to have been folded over before being driven on many times. Hector pried them open to see what the secret message from the universe would be. But it wasn't a secret message. It was a girl's name. The bent letters spelled out *Debbie*.

Hector considered it, then put it in his shirt pocket, picked up his guitar, and headed up the hill. He could present it to Debbie Pelbry at the block party, as a sort of a joke. It could be funny. He could make her laugh.

CHAPTER 37
On the Roof

Having wandered aimlessly into the Karposkis'
backyard, someone noticed the ladder leaning
against the house. Almost but not quite without
thinking they climbed it, up onto the lower part of
the roof, then from there to the higher section of the
split-level roof. They sat up there like a flock of large
birds along the peak, roosting in the dark. Hector
had removed his sarong for easier climbing, and
wrapped it around his shoulders like a shawl.

The adults down at the block party floated through the mellow colored lights like fish in an aquarium. They moved into a conga line, each person's hands on the shoulders or hips of the person in front, winding around and bouncing. The music from the record player was blurred by the distance, so were their laughter and shouts. Watching was compelling and hypnotic, like gazing into a fire in the fireplace. Like children at the fireplace, the youths on the roof faced into the glow, their faces, shins, and forearms glowing, with darkness all around them. This cozy observation was made in the murky recesses of Hector's mind, and when he began singing "chestnuts roasting on an open fire" in a Mel Torme voice, even he didn't know why. But it seemed like a good idea. Everyone thought so. They all joined in.

Rowanne, who had parked the car next to the roadblock, walked up the dark street and heard Hector's voice above the others. She smiled to herself and followed it. When she reached the

Karposkis' house she saw them and, between verses, called up softly, How did you get up there? Someone called back about the ladder, and she went around and climbed up, too.

By that time the song was ending, and conversations sprouted along the roofline while they watched the party/aquarium/bonfire, or just enjoyed sitting on a roof in the dark, bracing themselves slightly on the rough shingles against the slant.

Hector asked Rowanne over his shoulder if they could stay a little longer and she said sure. Planting one foot up on the higher level, she hauled herself up onto an available space at the close end, beside Debbie, who said, "Hi."

Rowanne said, "Hi," too, and for a minute or so they sat there, quietly. Then Rowanne, who was more of a conversationalist, said, "So, how's it going? Are you having a good summer?"

"It's okay," said Debbie. "Parts of it have been pretty good."

"Oh, yeah?" said Rowanne. "Which parts?"

When Debbie hesitated, she said, "I bet they're romantic parts. Are they?"

"Maybe," said Debbie. "I'm not sure."

"I know what you mean," said Rowanne. "Sometimes it's pretty unclear. At least in my experience. Which I don't have that much of."

"Do you think," said Debbie, "that if someone comes into your life for a really short time and then disappears forever, that it counts?"

"Counts?" echoed Rowanne. "As what? As a romance?"

"I think that's what I mean," said Debbie.

"How short?" asked Rowanne. "Five minutes? An hour? A day?"

"A few days," said Debbie. "Three and a half days, spread out over a week."

"You're not talking about one of those carnival guys, are you?" asked Rowanne.

"No," said Debbie.

"I think it can count," said Rowanne. "I think everything counts."

"Do you know Miss Spransy?" asked Debbie. "The piano teacher? Actually, she's Mrs. Szebo now."

"I've heard her name," said Rowanne, "but I don't know her."

"I used to take lessons from her," said Debbie. "She lives in a tiny little house up in Birdvale. When I was taking lessons from her, her mother lived there, too. It was her mother's house. Her mother was pretty old, and Miss Spransy was getting older, too, I don't know how old. A little older than middle-aged, I think, but she had never gotten married, or even left home, as far as I know. I used to wonder about it; she was pretty, I thought. And you could tell she had been even prettier when she was younger. She had nice eyes, really kind eyes, and she was sort of skinny and elegant, although she was starting to thicken up around the middle and get wrinkly. She had kind of a long nose. She always wore a dress and dress shoes, and she always wore a cardigan with a little chain holding the front together but a few inches apart.

And she always had a folded Kleenex stuffed up her sleeve.

"I used to wonder if she had ever had a boyfriend. If she had gone out on dates when she was younger. I wondered if someone had broken her heart, and she could never love anyone again. Or maybe she had loved someone and he died.

"The piano was in their living room. The living room was tiny, and the piano was a baby grand. There was an organ in there, too. There were doilies and afghans everywhere. I think the two of them crocheted all the time.

"I remember seeing an article in the Sunday paper, about drawings and paintings made by people who were mentally ill. They showed pictures of four paintings that a mentally ill person had made, all of cats."

"I saw that," said Rowanne. "The first painting looked pretty normal; the cat looked like a cat. But as the person fell deeper into mental illness—it was schizophrenia, I think—there started to be jagged electric outlines around all of the shapes, and in each painting there were more and more of the jagged outlines in these wild, neon colors until the cat almost completely disappeared."

"Except for its eyes," said Debbie. "And its pointy ears."

"Right," said Rowanne. "They were bizarre. They were beautiful in a way so that you almost thought, 'Oh, this person is mentally ill, but it's okay, because they can live in their own world and make these beautiful paintings,' but then there was also something scary about the paintings so you knew that it was a scary world, and that the person needed to be rescued."

"That's true," said Debbie. "But I guess I wasn't thinking about the scary part—I was just thinking about the bright colors right next to each other so they made your eyes vibrate, and how the patterns became so complicated that you had to look to find the cat.

"Because I saw the article, and a couple of days later I went for my lesson, and when I walked in the door there were all the afghans everywhere, in fluorescent stripes and neon patterns, and with the white doilies on dark wood, and the patterns in the wallpaper and the rug and the upholstery fabric, Miss Spransy and her mother in their patterned dresses almost disappeared into the room. Until they moved. It reminded me of those paintings. It almost seemed like a form of camouflage."

Rowanne laughed. "Camouflage by afghan," she said.

"Something like that," said Debbie. "Anyway, I stopped taking piano lessons around then. I wasn't practicing, and it seemed silly to be paying for lessons. But a few months later old Mrs. Spransy died. And a few months after that, Miss Spransy got married. She got married to a truck driver she met at a bowling alley, maybe in her navy blue dress with tiny white polka dots and her folded Kleenex tucked up her sleeve. I couldn't imagine her picking up something heavy like a bowling ball, let alone throwing it. I couldn't imagine her striking up a conversation with some big bulky guy. Because he *was* a big bulky guy. He was a guy who said 'youse.'"

"Maybe someone introduced them," said Rowanne.

"Maybe," said Debbie. "But I remember thinking that it just didn't sound right. It didn't sound like a good match. But I went there one day— I think it was a Saturday morning and I had walked up to the library, and something came over me and I just thought I would knock on the door and say 'hi.'

"They were frying doughnuts and they invited me in. The husband's name was Art Szebo, and he was very jolly and friendly. And Miss Spransy, or now she was Mrs. Szebo, I guess, was very jolly, too. She seemed softer and rounder and bouncier. They were having the best time. I had fun, too. We all sat there sifting cinnamon sugar onto doughnuts as they came out of the deep fryer, and eating them. We ate this amazing amount of doughnuts.

"The house seemed different than before. There seemed to be less afghans and doilies, and there were man things around. Like work boots by the door and a thermos on the counter and a big plaid jacket. Also it was morning, so there was sunlight pouring in. But there was also a kind of life that wasn't there before.

"They had only been married six months when Mr. Szebo had a heart attack and dropped dead. Right at the bowling alley. When I heard about it, I felt terrible. I thought her life now would be so lonely and heartbroken and cold.

"But I saw her again, and she seemed still happy. Still soft and rounded and relaxed like she had been in the kitchen on the day we had doughnuts. And I think it's because she had been loved. Even though it wasn't for very long, maybe it was enough. Mr. Szebo hadn't left her or stopped loving her, there had been, like, a mechanical-technical failure. Something no one could help.

"This probably sounds stupid, I know I'm still young and there's a lot of time for things to happen, but sometimes I think there is something about me that's wrong, that I'm not the kind of person anyone can fall in love with, and that I'll just always be alone.

"But I think if I knew someone was going to fall in love with me when I'm fifty-three or something, I think I could wait. Maybe. If I knew it would at least happen."

Rowanne made a hmm sound in the back of her throat, without opening her mouth.

"I think everyone feels that way sometimes," she said. "It's not stupid."

For a minute or two they were quiet, then Rowanne said, "I have a story about love, too."

She paused, squinting a little as the story organized itself in her mind.

"There's a girl where I work," she said. "But first, I have to tell you about my job.

"It's just for the summer. Thank God, or I would shoot myself. Fifteen of us show up every morning at seven-thirty and we sit at rows of desks. Each of us has a stack of cards, and we sit there all day, eight hours, and type what's on the cards into the computers. You can say a few words to the person next to you, but there's a supervisor, Vicky, and she makes sure everyone keeps typing.

"There are no windows. You can't see out. It's like sensory deprivation, eight hours of typed cards, plywood walls, buzzing fluorescent lights, and wrinkled black carpet. And the radio. Every time a song comes on that I like, and I can feel my spirits lifting, Vicky switches it to something horrible and turns up the volume. Then I can hear everyone singing along while they type. They all like the same horrible music.

"Sometimes I go into the bathroom and just sit there in the cubicle, daydreaming that someone will drive up in a little red sports car and rescue me. When I leave, at four-thirty in the afternoon, I go out the door and the hot smelly air and the dirty sidewalk feel like beauty, and freedom. I want to kiss the pavement."

"Why do you keep working there?" asked Debbie. Rowanne seemed to her to be a person who would never let herself be stuck where she didn't want to be.

"I thought it would be better than waitressing," said Rowanne. "Now I'm not so sure. But I'm only there until the end of August. For most of them, this is it, this is life, it's what you do after high school. And they all pretty much think it's okay. Not great or

320

anything, but okay. Where if I thought this was it, I'd melt into a blithering idiot.

"We all bring our lunches and pull chairs up around a table in the front of the room and eat. You can go out, but there's only half an hour and you would have to spend money. Sometimes I do it anyway. But usually I sit there and eat my sandwich and listen to everyone talk about their boyfriends.

"They talk about their boyfriends all the time, and they talk about them as if they've been married for twenty years. I'm sort of a freak there because I don't have a boyfriend and I'm going to college. I think they feel sorry for me for both reasons. And because I have short fingernails.

"I used to try to join in the conversation, but my perspective is just too weird for them. The only topics where I've found I can speak pretty freely without blowing anyone's mind are the weather and food. I can say, 'I could just live on Fritos and Oreos,' and they're all with me. Because they're basically nice people, they want to include me. They just can't imagine why anyone would read a book of their own free will.

"So mostly I eat and listen to them talk.

"There's a girl there named Becky. At the beginning of the summer, she always talked about her boyfriend, Rick. My first reaction was, Wow, even Becky has a boyfriend, what's wrong with me? Because she's—you might call her a loser. I know that sounds mean, but, it's hard to put your finger on; she doesn't have a lot going for her. The lights are on, but nobody's home.

"So Becky would always say something about Rick and everyone would smile and nod and say, 'Oh, that's nice,' or if she was mad at Rick they would say, 'Oh, you shouldn't put up with that; tell him where he can go,' stuff like that. There was something odd about it, but I didn't think too much about it. The feeling I got was that no one really liked Rick, but they figured he was the best she could do.

"Then she told us all that she and Rick were getting married. She was quitting; Rick didn't want her to work. She gave two weeks notice; her last day would be a Friday. We had a little party for her that day after work. There was a cake, and we all chipped in to buy her some flimsy, frilly nightgown set. She was so happy, so excited. Then she was gone.

"But a couple of days ago, she was back at work. I figured Rick decided they needed two incomes after all. At lunch, I asked her how the wedding went. I'm thinking, Oh goodie, finally I get to say something besides 'I like food.' She seemed to . . . shrink, or melt a little bit and immediately everyone was talking about something else. I thought, uh-oh, something must have gone wrong; they must have had a fight or something. They had fights all the time.

"So a little later I went up to Vicky's desk to trade in my stack of cards for another one and I asked her, really quietly, 'Did Becky and Rick have a fight; did they not get married?'

"She looked at me as if I were a moron, a nice moron, and said, 'There isn't any Rick. She made it all up. She makes them all up.'

"It blew me away. They all knew, and they had a party for her; a cake, presents. And when she came back, because she had to, she needed the money, no one said a word.

"Now already she has another boyfriend. Now she talks about Tony all the time. And they all sit there and say, 'Oh, that's nice,' or whatever."

She hesitated.

"I think it's sad and pathetic that Becky feels like it's so important to have a boyfriend that she makes one up. I can see how she would feel that, I mean, I'm just in this place for a few months and I fall into it, I get lost in it a little bit. And it's those women, those girls (they're really some kind of a cross between girls and women) who do it to her, though not on purpose. I mean, I think it's all they know about.

"But, at the same time, I think there's something noble, something about love in how they go along with her. They give her dignity of some kind.

"Does that make any sense?" she asked. "Do you know what I mean?"

CHAPTER 38

Lightning Bugs

Other people on the roof were having conversations, too. It was the lightning bugs flickering all over the backyards that eventually drew them all back down the ladder. Someone went inside for a mason jar, someone put a little grass in it, someone went into a garage to tap air holes into the cap, and they moved around through the darkness in slow motion: watching, advancing, waiting, grabbing.

Debbie was holding the jar. She lifted the cap as

the capturers delivered their prey. Between deliveries she watched the bugs crawl and flutter around inside the jar, searching for the exit. It seemed cruel to keep them in there when it was so obvious that they wanted to get out. But she told herself that once they were free, their small, basic brains would probably have no memory of being imprisoned. Of their time in The Jar. She hoped this was true. In the meantime she might as well look closely at their red and black wings, lit up by their fellow lightning bugs, and watch their glow parts go on and off.

"What makes them light up?" she asked Lenny as he brought another victim (temporary, small brain) to the jar. She had the feeling she had probably asked him before, but she forgot the answer.

"It's a chemical reaction," he said. "In their abdomens."

"Why do they do it?" she asked.

"It's how the males find the females," said

Lenny. "There are different kinds in different parts of the world. There's one in South America that has red and green lights on the same bug. It's called a railway beetle because it looks like a train signal." Encyclopedia information. He still remembered a lot of it.

They were both looking into the jar. Then Lenny looked at Debbie's face, intent and summery in the wobbly light, and he thought of a question he could ask her.

"Wanna go to the movies?" he asked.

No one had ever asked Debbie this question before. She had imagined, often, being asked this question, but not by Lenny. He was the wrong person. Wasn't he? She had never felt that way about him.

Had she?

His question caught her off guard, and she didn't know what to do with it. The part of her that was open to the universe was facing in another direction just then. She felt disoriented and uncomfortable and there was Lenny, waiting for her to say something back.

"I think it's better if we're just friends," she said.

To her relief Patty arrived with a lightning bug. As she flicked it into the jar, Lenny said to her, "Do you wanna go to a movie?"

"Okay," she said. "What movie?"

Debbie wasn't sure what had just happened. She didn't know if she had gotten out of an awkward situation or invented one. Or missed an opportunity. She felt an impulse to say, "Can I go, too?" Instead she handed Patty the jar and said, "Can you hold this for a while? I'm going to go catch some."

But when she had walked away into the darkness, she just stood there.

Hector was lying on his back in the grass, looking up at the stars and playing his guitar. The sarong was bunched under his head for a pillow, and he was relying on the sound of his guitar and, near his head, a citronella candle he had borrowed from a local picnic table to keep from being stepped on.

He was thinking that maybe love was like starting a fire with two sticks. You've always heard that it's possible, but how likely is it?

Debbie came over and sat, cross-legged, on the grass nearby. She crossed her arms, too, at the wrist, her hands resting side by side on her ankle. She was thinking that happiness wasn't necessarily, as Dorothy in *The Wizard of Oz* says, in your own backyard. But it might be nearby, in someone else's backyard. She was thinking that the grass really could be greener on the other side of the fence. It depended on who was standing in the grass. Maybe you had to go take a look. Maybe she was the kind of person who would have to go Somewhere Else, and she wondered how far away Somewhere Else would have to be.

Her eyes were open, but it was dark. Except for lightning bugs and stars and Hector's candle. She listened to the guitar, which sounded perfect in the midsummer night air. Hector was doing pretty well for not being able to see and lying on his back. He was making up a song that didn't have anything to do with his life so far. That's what he liked about it. He didn't know where it had come from or what kind of a song it was. He was just messing around.

As usual, it wasn't a complete song. It was just the refrain, and it had a rhythm. It didn't quite have verses, or a melody, though it was trying to. To compensate for that, Hector sang it in a soft, twangy drone that was kind of a walk-through, a talk-through, as if, if he were really serious about singing it, there would be a melody there.

> It's a long, long road
> I'm a-goin', goin' home
> I am goin' by myself
> I am goin' on my own
> I can't say I'll never leave there
> I can't say I'll never roam
> 'Cause my heart don't grow in soil
> not the deepest darkest loam
> Just that berm on
> the side of
> the road . . .

After listening for a few minutes, Debbie hummed along, then sang it with him as she picked up the words. She sang a harmony, which was interesting seeing as how there wasn't even a melody yet. She listened as Hector fooled around with the chords, looking for a verse, then she said,

"Wait, I have one." Hector listened while she sang:

> Going somewhere, having gone
> I see I still must travel on
> I come and go, I go and come
> And will for all my journey on
> that long, long road
> and I'm goin', goin' home (etc.)

This was the refrain again and Hector came back in. The melody was clearer now. Their voices rose and fell, separated and came back together, like two birds flying just for fun. That's what they were doing, more or less.

At some point Hector had shifted up to a sitting position, and now he remembered the necklace. He stopped playing, abruptly, and fished around in his pocket.

"I almost forgot," he said. "I have a gift for you."

"A gift?" said Debbie. "What for?"

He drew the necklace out and held it suspended

in the light of the citronella candle. Debbie let out a noise of surprise.

"I had it made especially for you," said Hector. "I had cars drive over it."

"That's my necklace," said Debbie. "Where did you find it?"

She took the necklace and looked at the battered letters of her name. Ouch. The tiny red gem that had dotted the *I* was gone. The catch was completely busted.

"I'm glad it's not a voodoo necklace, or I would be in really bad shape," she said.

"I think you should wear it," said Hector. "It's like one of those dogs that travels a thousand miles to get back to its owner."

"I can't," said Debbie. "The little thing is broken."

"I'll tie it in a knot," said Hector. "Lean over."

Debbie wondered briefly how she would get it off later, but she leaned over and let Hector tie a knot in the gold chain. As she leaned over, she pulled her hair away from her neck and let it hang down in a waterfall, a temporary cave, around her face. She could feel Hector's fingers fumbling with the flimsy chain at the back of her neck.

Hector, suddenly aware of Debbie's hair and her neck in this unaccustomed arrangement and closeness, became clumsy. It took him forever to tie the knot. Finally he did it, and she raised her head and her hair went back down in the usual way, but floofed up and disheveled from having been upside down.

Her loose hair, her summeriness, the existence of the back of her neck, and something she was in the process of learning made her look different than she had a few months ago. She sensed that she herself had something to do with the good and different and important thing that had happened to her, but she didn't know how she had done it, or how to do it again. How much of it was luck. Thinking about this had changed the expression in her eyes.

As for Hector, he had spent a lot of time walking

lately. He had walked out of his roly-poly childhood, out of his cocoon. And he had spent a lot of time playing his guitar. It was a leaner, more thoughtful Hector who sat there in the cooling grass. He looked different, too.

There they were, both of them waking up on a midsummer night. There was even good lighting: the citronella candle.

Something should have happened. Maybe their eyes should have met, and they should have seen each other, really seen each other. After singing together like flying birds and tying on necklaces and all that.

Hector did look at Debbie, and he saw her, really saw her for a moment. Debbie looked at Hector and she saw him, really saw him, for a moment. If it had been the same moment, something might have happened. But their moments were separated by about a second. Maybe only half a second. Their paths crossed, but they missed each other.

The hardworking necklace couldn't believe it. It let out an inaudible, exasperated gasp.

Maybe it was another time that their moments would meet. Maybe it would happen in a few days, or next week. Maybe it would happen when they were fifty.

But just now they had missed, and the jet trails of the crisscrossing moments left an awkward vacuum in their wake. They both felt it, though they didn't know what it was, and when they tried to guess, they both got it wrong.

To fill it up, Debbie said, "Can you play another song?"

Hector pulled his guitar back onto his lap and started to play. He played "Greensleeves," because it was easy and sad and so beautiful.

Alas my love, you do me wrong.

The song was so old, but it was such a new, real feeling. They sang it together, but their thoughts went off to different places, to different people. Maybe the wrong places, the wrong people. How did anyone know? Mistakes would have to be made. Maybe a lot of mistakes. It was okay. They can't hear me, but I want to tell them it's okay, they're doing just fine.

Phil came over and sat down. Then Tesey. Rowanne. Lenny. Patty. Chrisanne. Phil's brother, Rick, and his sister Mary Angela. Were the Ciccolinis still there? The Doreskis? It's hard to remember. It was dark, but it seems as if they might have been. It felt like there were a lot of personalities sitting there in the grass. Separate in their thoughts, but together, too.

Someone opened the jar. The lightning bugs knew what to do. They flew out into the night air, every last one. Blinking, "Here I am."